He trailed her neck with his fingers, then let them linger on the diamond-and-emerald amulet.

"Is this the original?"

"Yes." The word was barely a whisper. His face was so close. She couldn't fight this. The attraction was too unexpected and far too overpowering. "It was found and returned to us."

"It's beautiful. You're beautiful."

And then he kissed her. The world began to spin as if she were on a mad carousel. She kissed him back, over and over until every part of her was lost in the passion and need.

A siren sounded in the distance. He pulled away. "I have to go. Tomorrow night in the ballroom. Same time?"

She nodded. His hand trailed her arm one last time, as if he hated to leave her.

She wanted to see him tomorrow night, and the night after, and every night for as long as she could.

But how long would he stay around once he knew the truth about her?

JOANNA WAYNE
THE AMULET

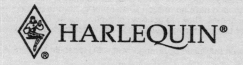

HARLEQUIN®

TORONTO • NEW YORK • LONDON
AMSTERDAM • PARIS • SYDNEY • HAMBURG
STOCKHOLM • ATHENS • TOKYO • MILAN • MADRID
PRAGUE • WARSAW • BUDAPEST • AUCKLAND

ISBN 0-373-22888-0

THE AMULET

Copyright © 2005 by Jo Ann Vest

www.eHarlequin.com

Printed in U.S.A.

ABOUT THE AUTHOR

Joanna Wayne lives with her husband just a few miles from steamy, exciting New Orleans, but her home is in the perfect writer's hideaway. A lazy bayou, complete with graceful herons, colorful wood ducks and an occasional alligator, winds just below her back garden. When not creating tales of spine-tingling suspense and heart-warming romance, she enjoys reading, traveling, playing golf and spending time with family and friends.

Joanna believes that one of the special joys of writing is knowing that her stories have brought enjoyment to or somehow touched the lives of her readers. You can write Joanna at P.O. Box 2851, Harvey, LA 70059-2851.

Books by Joanna Wayne

CAST OF CHARACTERS

Katrina O'Malley—She has one thing on her mind until she meets the handsome detective who teaches her what love is all about.

Deputy Bart Finnegan—He's no longer officially on the murder case, but he's got too much at stake to give it up.

Deputy Carrie Fransen—After her partner gets shot, she's spooked over the ghostly happenings that no one can explain.

Deputy Dick McFarland—He's your typical, arrogant, controlling deputy—and Carrie's new partner.

Maisie Henderson—She runs a small café and knows a lot about everybody.

Tom Henderson—What he's seen in the mountains may have blown his mind forever.

Owen Billings—He's very protective of his troubled wife.

Selma Billings—She's depressed over her miscarriage—and suspected of having a ghostly experience of her own.

Jeff Matthews—He's a travel photographer whose pictures tell a frightening story.

Harlan Grant—He's done time for a sex-related crime, but is he guilty now?

Marjorie Lipscomb—A renowned psychologist who had an eerie and mysterious experience while staying at the Fernhaven Hotel.

Elora Nicholas—The victim who was raped and killed the night Bart Finnegan was shot.

Prologue

Visibility was next to zero in the thick fog, and the roads were wet and icy from the light sleet that had started falling about ten minutes earlier. It was the kind of night a man should be sitting in front of the fire, cuddled up with some sweet young thing and sipping wine. It was not a night for driving deadly mountain roads.

The going was slow, and the steep, winding road seemed to go on forever before Bart Finnegan finally caught a glimpse of the lights from the Fernhaven Hotel. The place seemed to erupt from the mountain and soar to the sky. And somewhere inside the vast, castlelike structure, a man was looking for his wife and afraid she'd met with foul play.

Hotel security had taken him seriously enough they'd called the sheriff's department. Bart had heard the call when it came through and volunteered to investigate even though he was already off duty.

He made the sharp curve to the right. The impressive hotel was in full sight now. Shrouded in the mist, it looked like something straight from a horror novel. He lost sight of the hotel again as he wound through the expansive grounds.

He knew there were secluded guest cabins out there somewhere, but he couldn't see them in the dark. He rounded another sharp curve and something moved into the beam of his headlights before disappearing. Probably an animal of some kind, but instinctively, his hands tightened on the wheel and he pulled to the shoulder.

He didn't see anything in the glow of the flashing red and blue lights, so he lowered his window and aimed his high-powered flashlight into the wooded area. No sign of movement, but still he climbed out of the car for a better look. And that's when he spotted what looked to be two people darting from one tree to another.

Adrenaline hit and he reached back in the car to grab the loud speaker as he palmed his weapon.

"Police. Identify yourself and your business on the property."

The response was a bullet that ricocheted off the front fender of his squad car. Damn. He had a nut on his hands. Bart aimed his gun, but didn't fire. A reckless shot wouldn't do anything but antagonize the shooter, and if the second figure happened to be the missing woman, it might put her in more danger.

Taking cover behind the car, he scanned the area with the flashlight once again. When he didn't see movement, he turned it off, knowing it would make him a target when he moved from behind the vehicle.

He took off in the direction the figures had disappeared, using the light from the police flashers to guide him. The land was rocky, wet and icy in spots, making maneuvering difficult. He traveled a few yards, then leaned against a tree and listened for a rustle of grass, the dry crushing of leaves beneath a boot, the sound of breathing, anything. And then as if she knew he was seeking a sign, the woman screamed.

Bart moved toward the sound, though he'd reached the outer edges of the flashers' illumination and was moving in almost total darkness. He didn't know this particular area, but he knew the dangers of the Cascades. They were riddled with drop-offs. One wrong step and a man—or woman—could wind up at the bottom of a cliff with a crushed skull.

Bart stopped again, took a deep breath and made a quick decision, hopefully the right one.

"We have you surrounded," he called from his spot behind the thick, protective trunk of a towering tree. "Give the woman up before the shooting starts and this will go a lot easier on you."

There was no answer, but Bart heard noises coming from his right. From the sound, he'd guess the man was dragging the victim along. The decline grew steeper, making footing even more treacherous on the icy ground. His foot slipped on a rock, and he had to grab a low-hanging branch to keep from falling. The branch snapped and crashed to the ground, telegraphing his position.

He darted for cover as the sound of gunfire cracked through the cold air. The bullet dug into his flesh. The pain was intense, ripping through his stomach like the blade of a hunting knife. He fell over, tasted dirt and blood and felt his insides rattle against his backbone.

And then he felt nothing at all.

Chapter One

One month later

Bart Finnegan stood at the window and looked down on the lush foliage that bordered the west lawn of Fernhaven Hotel. The evergreens were dusted with white as was the grass. They'd had heavy snows up higher in the mountains, but all they'd gotten at this altitude was a few flakes.

He'd have preferred a real snow. The dusting reminded him of the powdered sugar his stepmother used to put on cakes in lieu of icing. Cakes without icing were like peanut butter sandwiches without jelly. She'd put those in his lunch tin on several occasions as well.

Odd to be thinking about that now. He hadn't seen the woman or his father in years. Once he'd joined the Marines at eighteen, he'd pretty much put them and his past life behind him. It had been easier than he'd expected. Enemy bullets had been less scathing than his father's constant criticism and his stepmother's nagging.

A young couple rode by on the bike path that bordered one of the several creeks that ran through the property. They were dressed for the activity, in matching red and navy jogging suits and navy ski caps. Her long dark hair flowed behind her, even though she didn't seem to be pedaling all that fast. The man kept turning his head around as if to make sure she was still behind him.

They were the first people Bart had seen since he'd taken this room in the west wing. Actually, the wing wasn't even open yet, which was why the room was available. The rest of the hotel was sold out. *If you build it, they will come.*

The familiar phrase played in Bart's mind. He'd never have believed that the statement would have been true of a hotel built in a secluded part of the Cascade mountains. But, apparently, the rich and famous could be drawn anywhere that they believed was the *in* place of the winter season, even if a female guest had been raped and murdered only a month earlier.

But then thanks to the press, most people believed she'd been killed by her husband. They were wrong.

Bart was not one of the rich and famous drawn to the hotel to see and be seen. That's why the room in the unfinished wing fit him to perfection. The price was right, and the other hotel guests wouldn't even know he was around unless he chose to mingle with them.

Neither would the sheriff's department. As far as they were concerned, the gunshot wound had left him out of commission and there was no way they would ever have okayed his searching for the perp.

So he'd slip in and out of his isolated room and investigate on his own, roam the halls, listen in on conversations, nose around where he had no business. The old rules didn't apply anymore. What the sheriff's department didn't know couldn't hurt him.

CARRIE FRANSEN stared at Sheriff Huey Powell, trying desperately to hold her temper, a skill she'd never been good at. "Why Rich McFarland?"

"You can't work homicide without a partner. It's a department rule."

"I've heard you say more than once that rules are made to be broken."

"Not this one." He raked his fingers through his thin gray hair. "I know how close you were to Bart. That's why I left you alone for this long, but it's time to move on. You have to take a partner on this case."

"Then give me Kirk."

The sheriff shook his head. "Can't do that, not after what I received in the mail today." He took a clear plastic bag from the top of his desk and handed it to her. "I'm sending it out for a fingerprint check, but you can see it for yourself."

Stop me before I kill again.

There was no signature, but the logo of Fernhaven Hotel was taped to the bottom of the note. The logo looked as if it had been torn from one of the cocktail napkins they used in the lounge.

"It could be a hoax," she said.

"Could be, and I hope it is," Powell agreed. "But we can't ignore it. That's why I need Rich on this case. Other than me, Rich's got more years in law experience than anyone else in the department. Not only that, but he worked homicide in Seattle for ten years. We need that expertise on this case."

"It's taken weeks to get the people in the area to open up to me. If Rich goes in there with his tough guy, big-city cop routine, they'll crawl back into their reclusive hideaways and refuse to give us the time of day."

"You have more than the natives to deal with. You have the hotel staff and the guests that were there that weekend. As far as I know you haven't ruled out anyone yet."

"Not officially."

"Unofficially?"

"Not unofficially, either," she admitted.

"Then we're wasting our time here. You're working with Rich on this case. I'll let him know this afternoon. Fill him in on what you have and take him up to the hotel and introduce him around."

So that was it. A new partner—whether she liked it or not. And it would have to be the one guy in the department she'd cross the street in the rain just to avoid having to speak to him. The guy was just too arrogant for words.

Bart would laugh his head off if he were standing here right now. Only if he were here, none of this would be happening.

Sheriff Powell stood and stepped from behind his desk. He put a hand on her back between her shoulder blades. Not a hug. Not a clap like he would have given one of the other deputies. She was his only female deputy, and she was pretty sure the gender difference made him uncomfortable.

She didn't get it, but the sheriff was pushing seventy, and he saw a lot of things differently than she did.

She could hold her own, and she'd put her shooting skills against Rich McFarland's any day of the week. Bart had made sure of that. He'd gone with her to the shooting range several times a month, insisted that when it was crunch time, it was cop instinct and shooting accuracy that made the difference between life and death.

And sometimes even that wasn't enough.

THE NIGHT SPARKLED with tiny white lights that winked and blinked from the tall, stately spruce trees that dotted the grounds in front of the hotel, all part of the Christmas decor.

"Pretty impressive," Rich said. He slowed before they reached the circular drive where a crew of bell-men waited.

"Is this your first time to the hotel?" Carrie asked.

"I've been up here a couple of times since they finished it, but always in the daytime. The place looks different at night."

"Is that why you wanted to wait until dark to drive up here?"

"Partly. I also had some other business to take care of this afternoon."

He didn't explain what else he had to do, and she didn't ask.

"Hard to believe that a year ago, there was nothing here but woods and a few bricks from the fire-places of a hotel that burned to the ground over seventy years ago," she said, once again marveling at the grandeur of the hotel.

Rich nodded. "Harder to believe someone built a hotel in the exact same spot. Obviously they weren't superstitious, which means they were probably not from around here."

"No, but the woman who rebuilt it was a descen-dant of the original builder. She meant it as a monument to her ancestor and the past. That's why she built almost an exact replica."

"Kind of like the *Titanic Two*," Rich said. "But from the looks of that parking lot it must not matter."

He slowed as he reached the circular drive.

"I guess we should introduce you to the night security supervisor before we do anything else," Carrie said.

"I'd like to see the spot where they found the woman's body," Rich said, making a U-turn and heading back the way they'd come.

"Tonight?"

"Seems as good a time as any."

She tried to count to ten silently, but only made it to eight. "They found the body at the bottom of a ravine."

"So?"

"It's pitch-dark out there."

"You scared of the dark, Fransen?"

"Of course not. I just don't see the point in roaming the woods at night when I've thoroughly examined the scene in the daylight and documented all my findings. You have read the reports, haven't you?"

"I read them, but I like to see things for myself."

"You can't see a lot in the dark."

"I'll see what the perp saw that night. And what

the woman saw before she was raped, branded and murdered."

"It's not safe to hike that area in the dark."

"Must be why they made flashlights."

Smart-ass, she mouthed, her gaze straight ahead.

"You know if I didn't know better, Fransen, I'd think those ghost tales had gotten to you and that you're afraid to go into the woods at night."

"Nice you know better." But the comment got her attention. "I haven't heard any ghost tales."

"Then you must not be talking to the right people. The locals up here claim this area of the Cascades is inhabited by the undead."

"The undead?"

"That's what they say."

"And exactly what are the undead?"

"You'll have ask someone who believes that bull for the definitive answer, but according to Maizie Henderson they are referring to people who are no longer living, but not gone from this dimension."

She didn't know a Maizie Henderson. "I've talked to a number of locals during the course of the investigation. No one mentioned ghosts to me."

"They're not big on talking about their superstitions, especially to outsiders."

"And just how would you know that, Mr. Seattle cop?"

"My grandparents lived just a few miles from here up until my parents moved them to an assisted living facility in Seattle a few months ago. My grandfather was big into mountain lore."

Great. Now Rich was not only the authority on homicide, he was also the authority on the locals. She wasn't sure why that irritated her so, but it did.

He slowed to a crawl. "Aren't we near the spot where Bart stopped that night?"

"Just around the next curve."

He took the curve, then pulled off the road and killed the engine and the headlights. A blast of cold air hit her in the face when he opened his door. She grabbed her parka from the back seat, and pulled it on as she stepped out of the car. An owl hooted somewhere above her and something rustled the grass a few feet away.

"Ready to hike?" Rich asked, cutting away a wide swath of black with the bright beam of his flashlight.

All of a sudden she had the bizarre but almost overwhelming feeling that someone was watching them. But it couldn't be. She and Rich were the only living souls around. "I'm ready," she lied.

He handed her a flashlight. "Want to lead the way?"

"Sure." Lead the way right past the spot where Bart had been shot. Right to the ravine where Elora Nicholas's body had been found, her stomach branded with some weird design. She breathed in a huge gulp of cold night air and started walking. She would not be spooked by the dark or ghost tales. Or by the icy tingles climbing her spine.

IT WAS ten past nine when Bart took the service elevator to the first floor, then followed the strains of a waltz to the Glacier Ballroom. According to information in the hotel lobby, the ballroom was the site of fabulous Christmas balls held every Saturday night in December. The soirees were acclaimed as a not-to-be-missed activity, and Bart had no intention of missing this one.

Not that he was into balls, but it was an excellent opportunity to check out the guests, at least sixteen of whom also had been guests the night the woman had been abducted, and he'd been shot. Apparently, people couldn't get enough of this place. Considering the prices they charged, he found that pretty amazing.

But then the hotel did have an ambiance he hadn't expected. Elegant, yet the staff was warm and friendly. Breathtaking scenery, rugged yet serene. Remote, but there was a shuttle that made a run a few times a day to the ski trails an hour northwest of here.

He adjusted the jacket of the black suit he'd "borrowed" from the servant supply closet on the first floor. The fit wasn't great, but it would do for a waiter. For the most part he hoped to go unnoticed amid the party crowd. He was here to observe and overhear, not to be seen.

The ballroom was already crowded when he followed a middle-aged couple through the open double doors. Men in black tuxes and women in elegant dresses that swept the polished wood floor filled the dance floor and sat at white-clothed tables listening to the music and sipping champagne.

Huge crystal chandeliers hung from the domed ceiling, and everywhere he looked there were huge bouquets of flowers and tables of food accented with delicately carved ice statues. It was a far cry from his usual Saturday night burger and a couple of beers at Jake's Bar and Grill.

The band started a new number, this time a tune he recognized, though he didn't know the name of it. A woman walked past him, close enough that the silky fabric of her gown brushed his fingers and the fragrance of her perfume crawled inside him and evoked a memory he'd thought was dead and buried.

It got to him a lot more than it should have. He took a few steps backward, then stopped, mesmerized by a woman across the room.

Her hair was the color of molten gold, though the strands that caught the glow of the chandeliers took on a reddish tint. It was piled high on top of her head, with curly tendrils falling about her cheeks and forehead.

Her dress was emerald-green, cut low enough to show cleavage. It fit tightly around her tiny waist, then swirled into yards of satin that didn't stop until they reached the floor. But the jewel of the outfit hung from a silver chain around her neck, a huge emerald surrounded by pale yellow diamonds. He'd never seen anything so spectacular in all his life.

He looked around, half-expecting the rest of the people to be staring at her the way he was. They weren't. They were dancing, filling crystal flutes with the champagne that bubbled from a fountain or snaring delicacies from the trays of waiters who meandered the ballroom.

Only he seemed to be enchanted by the woman, and not just by her physical appearance and the pendant. She had an ethereal quality about her that made it seem as if she were more dream than reality.

He started toward her. A middle-aged woman in red bumped into him. Her champagne spilled and dripped onto his slacks and the toe of his shoes. He bent to brush it off. When he looked up again the woman in the emerald gown had disappeared.

He hurried across the room, searching the crowds for a glimpse of her. When he didn't find her, he pushed through the double doors that led to the garden. Still no sign of her.

Yet somehow he knew he'd see her again.

Chapter Two

The cold sneaked into Carrie's lungs as she and Rich tramped the near frozen ground. The mountains had a whole different feel at night. Eerie shapes coalesced in the mist, and crept across the rugged terrain at the far edges of their flashlight beams like translucent shadows.

The decline grew sharper, and she had to grab on to the trunks of spindly trees or to low-hanging branches to keep her balance as her boots crashed through the layers of leaves, twigs and exposed roots.

"I still can't imagine why the man dragged Elora all the way out here to kill her," Carrie said.

"Maybe he wasn't planning on killing her. He may have been taking her somewhere, then panicked when he crossed paths with Bart."

"Taking her where?"

"Maybe a mountain hideaway or an old cave. It might have been a kidnapping that turned deadly."

Could have been, but she hadn't uncovered any evidence to indicate that was the case. "The body was found over there," she said, aiming the beam of her flashlight at the ravine just past a downed tree. There were still remnants of the yellow crime scene tape. The rest had been blown away.

Rich stepped over the trunk of the fallen tree, then shot a beam of light into the ravine.

Carrie stayed back. "You're not crawling down in the ravine, are you?"

"No, I can see enough from here. Mainly I wanted to get a feel for what it was like out here in the dark. It helps me put myself in the killer's shoes."

"I don't know about the killer, but I'm sure Elora must have been terrified."

"Yet she apparently didn't make enough fuss when they left the hotel that anyone noticed."

"He probably had a gun to her head. She may have even been gagged."

"Or she may have known him. I'm sure you checked for any sign of a lover's triangle."

"I checked. Not even a hint of one."

"And the husband checked out."

"I didn't find any reason to suspect him. If anything he seemed very much in love with her. He'd even blown his Christmas bonus to bring her here for their tenth anniversary."

Carrie was certain Rich would check all this out for himself, if he hadn't already. He was just getting her take on the details, probably to find fault with it.

"But they'd argued just before she disappeared?"

"He wanted another drink and she wanted to go back to the room so she could call and check on the kids. She stormed off, and that was the last time she was seen alive."

"But one of the shoes she was wearing was found by the back service entrance?"

"Right."

"Have you got any leads on those markings the killer carved into her stomach?"

"No. One squiggly line intersected by a straight one, but not at right angles."

"Yeah. I've seen the crime scene photos," Rich said. "Still hard to figure. He had a gun, so why kill the woman by slitting her throat?"

"And then throw her into a ravine," Carrie added.

"That made sense. Like the condom he used, the water would make it more difficult to collect DNA evidence."

Carrie stamped her feet a few times to warm them. "It's almost like the type of pattern you'd find from a serial killer."

"Or someone who'd given this crime a lot of thought before he committed it. Be nice if someone had found either the gun or the knife."

"Agreed. We have the bullet that hit the squad car. It was from a .38."

Crazy, but she almost felt guilty talking to Rich about this case. Bart had been the only partner she'd ever worked with. He'd taken her on when she was so green she didn't even know her way around a warrant. He was her mentor, her friend, her...

"Had to be a man who not only knew about evidence, but also knew his way around the mountains and around the hotel," Rich said, breaking into her troubling thoughts. "A stranger to these parts would never have taken off through the woods on a pitch-dark night. Reminds me of some other murders that occurred near here a few years back."

Damn. She didn't know about any other murders. Not one person had mentioned them, not even Sheriff Powell.

"A serial killer?"

"No. A mass slaughter. Four female campers had their throats cut one summer night. Two were found in the tent, apparently killed while they slept. The other two were killed in the surrounding woods. It appeared they'd tried to run away, but the lunatic had chased them down."

"How long ago did that happen?"

"Twenty years or so. I was in junior high. It made quite an impression on me at the time."

"What happened to the killer?"

"He was never officially apprehended, but some transient who'd been sleeping at the camp grounds killed himself a few days later, and most thought he'd done it from guilt."

"I'm surprised the sheriff hasn't mentioned those murders in view of the present investigation."

"Why? No reason to think there's any connection between those and what we're dealing with." He rested one foot on the trunk of the downed tree and lifted his head as if studying the dark haze that surrounded them. "Ready to head back to the car and a little warmth?"

She nodded, but the campsite killings stayed on her mind during the hike back, making the woods feel more eerie than ever.

Rich didn't talk at all until they reached the car. "See, that wasn't so bad," he said, opening his door and sliding behind the wheel.

"Not bad at all," she lied. "I found the mountain air invigorating."

And she missed Bart so much it hurt.

THREE DAYS LATER, Bart had still not run into the woman who'd mesmerized him in the ballroom. He had seen Rich McFarland several times, however—always at a distance.

It galled him that Rich had replaced him as Carrie's partner. This should have been his case all the way. He wouldn't interfere with what they were doing, but he wouldn't let them interfere with what he had to do, either. And he'd keep an eye on Carrie the way he'd done since the day he'd taken her on as a partner.

She was smart, but she still had a lot to learn. Not the kind of things you could learn from books. She'd aced all of that in her classes at the university. The knowledge she lacked was the kind that came from experience.

Bart had gotten his experience the hard way, working his way up the L.A.P.D. He didn't miss it anymore—at least not often. He breathed a lot better in the Cascades.

The sun was fighting its way through the early-morning haze when he took the service elevator to the first floor and slipped into the garden. It was too cold for blossoms, but the maze of perfectly manicured shrubbery still made for some interesting scenery.

Besides, if he went all the way to the far south corner, he could watch the arriving employees and the departing night staff. You could learn a lot by seeing who left in groups and who took off alone.

The garden was empty except for an older woman sitting on one of the stone benches. She looked to be at least in her seventies with paper-thin skin and deep wrinkles around her mouth and eyes. A full, dark skirt hung to her ankles revealing only a glimpse of her black leather boots. A woolen cloak shrouded her, covering her head, but he could see enough of her hair to tell it was gray.

She looked up when he approached. "Good morning, sir."

"Good morning. What brings you out so early?" he asked, mostly making small talk, but somewhat curious as to why she was out and about before the sun had cleared the horizon.

"I like to watch the sunrise from the garden."

"Do you come here often?"

"Too often."

A strange answer, but he wasn't about to pry into her business. "Enjoy your day," he said, in way of goodbye. He'd already walked by her when she responded.

"He'll kill again."

Bart stopped and spun around, wondering if he'd heard her wrong. "What did you say?"

"He'll kill again."

"Who'll kill again?"

"The man who abducted the woman and shot you."

The statement threw him off. He'd been certain no one knew who he was or why he was here. "How do you know who I am?"

"I listen."

That didn't explain much, but his thoughts were rushing ahead. "Do you know who abducted the woman?"

"No. Why are you looking for him?"

"I just want to find him and make certain he goes to prison before he strikes again."

"Is that your duty?"

"That's the way I see it."

She nodded and pulled her cloak tighter. "Maybe you should reconsider your priorities."

She stood and walked to a nearby fountain. Slowly, she slipped off her gloves and stuffed them into her skirt pockets. She spread her open arms in front of the spray the way people held their hands in front of the fireplace to get them warm. After a few seconds, she pressed her damp fingers to her thin lips.

"He kills because of what was done to him." Her voice was low and she was still facing the fountain, more as if she were muttering to herself than talking to him. He stepped toward her.

"You seem to have given the killer a lot of thought."

"No, but the mist is full of whispers."

Bart was beginning to doubt the woman was totally lucid, but she knew about him, so maybe she knew about other people as well. "I've been looking for a woman I saw the other night in the ballroom," he said. "She was wearing a long, green satin dress and a magnificent diamond-and-emerald pendant."

"Katrina."

"Is that her name?"

"Yes."

"Do you know her room number?"

"No, but if you watch for her, you'll see her again."

"What's her last name?"

"Katrina is all I know."

"Is she here with someone."

"No. She is always alone."

He heard voices on the path just beyond the garden. He checked his watch. Ten before six. The first of the day crew were arriving. The restaurant opened at seven, but room service ran all night, and the silver urn in the foyer was filled with hot coffee at exactly six-thirty every morning.

When he turned around again, the old woman was gone. But at least now he had a name for the mysterious woman. "Katrina." He said the name out loud, liking the sound of it as it rolled off his tongue.

Katrina. Beautiful. Elusive. And much too enchanting to spend her nights all alone.

CARRIE PUSHED UP the sleeve of her uniform and glanced at her watch. Only eight-thirty, and Rich was already getting on her nerves. It was the third day into the partnership, and she was still desperately searching for a sign it might actually work.

"I've already questioned half these people," she said, tossing the list of names he'd just handed her to the top of his desk. The same way she'd already questioned Elora Nicholas's husband, but Rich had spent the past two days putting the poor guy through an intensive interrogation.

"So, we'll talk to them again."

Her hands flew to her hips in spite of her determination not to butt heads with him today. "So what's the problem? Do you think I don't know how to handle a few questions?"

"I didn't say that."

"Then what makes you think we need to redo everything I've done for the past month."

"The case isn't solved, and we've got a killer out there threatening to strike again."

Like she needed him to point that out to her.

Rich picked up his coffee mug, an ugly green one with the logo of a Seattle pharmacy emblazoned across it in black. He took a long sip, then pushed back from his desk and grabbed his jacket. "You got a better idea for how to spend the day, Fransen, or do you just want to sit around here and jaw about it?"

"*Jaw* about it?"

"Okay." He gave a mock bow. "Is it your wish, Deputy Fransen, that we remain at the office and discuss this matter further?"

"It's my *wish* that we not waste time backtracking."

"So, what do you have in mind?"

"I know the hotel owners won't like it, but I think

it's time to start tracking down all the guests who were staying at the hotel that night."

"According to your notes, you already ruled them out."

"I did cursory background checks on all of them," she said, "but I think we should interrogate some of them further."

"For what purpose? The only red flags you reported were James Fox from Portland, a one-time shoplifting charge from twenty years ago, and Bailey Ledlow who did time for embezzlement."

So he had at least read her notes. Which meant he knew she'd talked personally to both of those men and was reasonably sure they weren't involved in the abduction. Ledlow was seventy years old and in poor health. He probably couldn't have made the hike through the woods alone, much less dragging a woman. James Fox and his wife had argued that weekend and checked out of the hotel early. They'd been back in Portland by the time Elora Nicholas had been abducted. Besides, neither of their prior crimes made them suspects in a murder case.

Rich walked to the door. "You going with me, or not?"

"Partners usually discuss their day."

"I thought that's what we just did."

He would. She started to point out that he was a jerk, then decided against it. Even if she argued and won her point, he was probably right. The killer was probably still here on the scene. Why else would they have received the note?

So they'd do this his way today. She'd just take advantage of this opportunity to sit back and watch McFarland in action, see if he had anything on her when it came to questioning the locals.

"Come on," Rich said. "I'll buy you breakfast."

"At the hotel?"

"At ten dollars an egg? Dream on."

She stopped at her office to grab her parka and to stick the copies of old police records from the camp-ground slaughter into a manila folder. They were another dead end. The transient who'd killed himself was the likely killer and there had been no similar crimes in the area since then.

Rich was already running down the two flights of stairs to the ground floor by the time she reached the hallway. She took the elevator, hoping she'd beat him down. It was the principle of the thing. She didn't. So much for principles.

CARRIE HAD BEEN to the area many times since signing on as deputy two years ago. She'd never been to or even seen the wind-and-weather mangled sign that said Maizie's Café. In fact, she'd never known this road existed. From the highway, it looked more like a dirt trail leading to someone's barn.

Turned out there were half a dozen or more houses and at least that many mobile homes tucked back in the trees along the dirt road that dead-ended at Maizie's. The sign and the array of mud-encrusted pickup trucks parked in a square of gravel where the yard should have been were the only indication this wasn't just another residence.

The house was a one-story, wood cottage that needed a paint job. A big gray cat was perched in a squeaking porch swing.

"How did you ever find this place?" Carrie asked, friendlier now that breakfast was beaconing.

"The third house on the left after you leave the highway is where my grandparents lived."

"I didn't notice. You'll have to point it out as we leave."

"Not much to see. Just an old house, about like this one."

"Who lives there now?"

"No one." He put the patrol car in Park, then climbed from behind the wheel. She followed, enticed by mouthwatering odors wafting on the slight breeze. He waited until she reached the porch before opening the restaurant door.

Once inside, she was hit with a new wave of the tantalizing odors she'd smelled from outside. She shrugged out of her parka and hung it over one of the hooks by the door while a chorus of gravelly voiced how-you-been's greeted Rich.

Okay, so he did know his way around the area. She'd give him that one. She looked for an empty table. There wasn't one, so she waited while Rich stopped at a couple of tables to *jaw.*

"You still looking for the guy who shot the cop and abducted that woman?" a man asked.

"Still looking," Rich admitted.

"I knew there would be trouble when they rebuilt that fancy hotel," another said. "Got strangers running these roads all hours of the day and night now."

Rich gave a noncommittal nod. A young waitress passed carrying a plate of bacon, eggs and biscuits.

"There're tables in the back room, Rich."

"Thanks, Jen."

"Obviously you're a regular in here," Carrie said as they found a table in the next room, one that was most likely the original dining room of the house. It was right off the kitchen and had a couple of windows that offered a great view of the mountains.

"Not so often."

"You know the waitress by name."

"I've known Jen since she was in diapers. That's Maizie's granddaughter. She and her mother live in the mobile home next door."

A minute later, Jen stopped at their table with two glasses of water. "What can I get you?"

"I haven't seen a menu," Carrie said.

"No menus. We got all the usual. Pancakes, eggs, sausage, bacon, pork chops, biscuits, toast. Got some homemade blackberry jam, too."

"I'll take two eggs, over easy, some sausage and biscuits," Rich said. "And coffee."

"Same for me," Carrie said, imagining her arteries hardening as she said it. But she hadn't heard a lot of healthy choices among Jen's offerings.

A smiling woman who looked to be in her mid-forties served the coffee. "'Bout time you got in to see me," she said, smiling at Rich. "How's your grandmother? Is she adjusting any better?"

"A little. She still misses being home. And she misses you. She said to tell you hello."

"You tell her hello right back. I been thinking about trying to get down there to see here, but I don't like driving in Seattle. Too much traffic. Gets me all rattled."

"I'll drive you down one day. She'd love to see you. Dad would, too."

"How's his heart?"

"Still beating."

"You tell him that darn dog of his still won't sleep here. He comes down to eat, but then he goes right back up there. Sleeps on the front porch most of the day, right in front of the front door. He's waiting for 'em to come back home."

Rich introduced Carrie to Maizie Henderson. Maizie merely nodded at her, then looked back at Rich. "I got to get back to the kitchen before Tom lets my sausages burn."

"How is Tom?"

She shook her head, and the smile she'd been wearing caved into a frown. "He just ain't the same anymore, Rich. It's like his body's here, but his mind's still up there in the mountains somewhere. I just wish I knew what happened on that hunting trip."

"He's still never said?"

"No, but something happened up there. A man don't just go hunting a normal man and come home a zombie unless he's seen something."

The statement captured Carrie's attention, but she waited until Maizie had returned to the kitchen before questioning Rich.

"Is Tom Maizie's husband?"

"Yeah."

"What happened to him in the mountains?"

"Had a stroke, I expect, but you'd never get Maizie to buy anything that rational."

"Why not?"

"Easier to blame the mountains than his health, I guess."

Jen returned to the their table with the coffee and a couple of apple muffins on flowered saucers. "Just out of the oven," she said, setting a muffin down in front of each of them. "I'll bring some butter to go on them."

Carrie took one bite of the muffin and forgot everything else. The texture was light and fluffy and there was just enough nutmeg and cinnamon to make her taste buds sing.

Before they finished the muffins, Jen had returned with their breakfasts and more coffee. Carrie was halfway through her eggs and sausage and her stomach was sliding past full when her mind when back to Maizie's suspicions about what had happened to her husband.

She waited until Rich was finished and excused himself to go to the men's room before she walked back to the kitchen. Maizie was turning eggs on the grill. Jen was arranging biscuits on a plate. Tom was nowhere to be seen.

Maizie looked up when Carrie approached. "How was your breakfast?"

"Delicious. The muffins were to die for."

Maizie smiled. "Everybody seems to like them. It's the fresh apples."

Carrie waited until Jen left with a tray of food. "It must be hard on you taking care of this place by yourself now that your husband's ill."

"Hard enough. He helps some, when his mind is clicking in."

"It seems strange that he'd go off on a hunting trip and come back so…"

"Out of it. Just plain out of it," Maizie said, finishing her sentence when Carrie hesitated.

"Does he know who you are?"

"He knows. It just don't seem to matter none. It's like he's somewhere else in his mind."

It did sound as if he might have had a stroke, or Alzheimer's. "What do the doctors say?"

"They say he's had some minor strokes and that his heart's wearing out. They use a lot of big words and keep wanting to try a lot of drugs, but they don't know the mountains the way I do."

Maizie's voice dropped a decibel or two and her hand shook as she lifted an egg from the grill and slid it onto a waiting plate.

"What do you know about the mountains that frightens you so?" Carrie asked.

"You don't want to know."

The eeriness of the conversation was making the hairs on the back of Carrie's neck raise, but she did want to know. Not that she was superstitious or actually believed the mountains were inhabited by ghosts, but she needed to understand these people the way Rich did. It was important to the investigation. "What could happen to a man in the mountains?"

"Not just to a man. It can happen to anybody. Ask Selma Billings. She can tell you, 'cept she don't like to talk about it."

"Doesn't like to talk about what?"

Finally Maizie looked up from the eggs and met Carrie's gaze. Her wrinkled flesh had grown pale, and her eyes had taken on a guarded look, as if there were secrets behind them that she couldn't let escape. "Just don't get trapped up there when the mist is thick."

The temperature of Carrie's blood seemed to drop a degree or two.

"So this is where you got off to," Rich said, joining them in the kitchen.

For once, Carrie was glad to see him. "I just wanted to offer my compliments to the chef."

"It's just breakfast," Maizie said. "Anyone can cook an egg." She cracked a couple more onto the hot grill.

It was clear the discussion of the mist was over. Just as well. The whole idea of a man going hunting in the mountains and coming back a zombie was freaky. Really freaky.

But like Rich said, there was probably a medical explanation for Tom's condition, and it would have nothing to do with the mist.

They said goodbye and left the back way. Carrie slid into the front seat of the car, but her mind was stuck on the conversation with Maizie. She reached to the backseat and picked up the list of names Rich had shown her earlier. Selma Billings was near the bottom.

"I say we start the day's questioning with Selma Billings," she said.

Rich scowled. "Exactly what did Maizie tell you when the two of you were alone in the kitchen?"

"That I shouldn't get trapped in the mist. What happened to Selma Billings that she won't talk about?"

"Don't know. She doesn't talk about it."

"Don't brush me off, Rich. I don't believe in ghost tales any more than you do, but I need to know what we're up against with the locals."

"It's an old Indian legend." He pulled into the driveway of a gray clapboard house with a black mixed breed cur curled up on the front porch. The dog perked up, then uncurled and came loping toward them.

Rich jumped out of the car and greeted the dog like they were old pals, scratching him behind the ears while the dog's tail wagged like mad. The dog ate it up. Surprise. Who'd have thought dogs would like him?

"Yeah. Good to see you, too, Jackson," Rich said, still walking toward the house.

She got out of the car and followed Rich and the dog up the narrow walkway. Obviously they were at his grandparents' house. She wasn't sure why they'd stopped, but before they left she planned to hear the details of the Indian legend and find out why Maizie was convinced the mountains had supernatural powers.

Chapter Three

Rich's grandparents' house possessed a warmth that seemed to seep from the painted walls and the worn rugs themselves. The furniture was heavy and over-stuffed, made for settling into with a good book or a mug of hot chocolate. The coffee and end tables were knotty pine, possibly homemade.

It was different than the foster home where she'd grown up. Most of the furniture in the house had been off limits. She was pretty much ignored except when the social worker came to call. Then everything was rosy.

Rich took off his jacket and tossed it on top of a stack of newspapers on the coffee table. "Make yourself comfortable. I won't be but a few minutes. I need to check on a couple of things while I'm here."

"It looks as if your grandparents just stepped out for a few hours," Carrie said, running her fingers across the carvings on the back of a wooden rocker before draping her own jacket across the beautiful wood.

"In their mind they have," Rich said. "They think they're coming back as soon as Gramps gets his strength back from his last heart attack. It's the only way they'd agree to leave the place."

"Hello, Jackson," she said, bending to pet the dog who was nosing her leg and sniffing her fingertips. "You like the smell of Maizie's cooking, don't you, boy?"

Jackson licked her hand in answer.

"Don't they allow pets in the home where your grandparents are?"

"No, but even if pets were allowed, they wouldn't have taken Jackson."

"They can't just leave him out here by himself."

"He's not by himself. He's got the mountains and the neighbors."

"But he's grieving for your grandparents."

"Missing someone doesn't kill you. Being thrown into an environment where you can't run free might." He walked away, leaving her standing by the brick hearth and an enormous fireplace that still held the smell of wood smoke. On the opposite wall, three windows looked out on the mountains.

Haunted mountains where a man could go hunting and come back without his mind. She stared into the distance for a while, trying to make sense of Maizie's story. Finally, she gave up and went in search of Rich. She found him in the kitchen, replacing a bulb in the overhead light fixture.

She started to question the need for replacing bulbs in a house where no one lived, but decided what Rich did in his grandparents' house wasn't her concern. She rested her hands on the back of a kitchen chair. "Tell me more about the Indian legend."

He finished changing the bulb and climbed down from the chair he'd been standing on. "It's just a bunch of nonsense."

"Like what?"

"It has variations. Which one do you want?"

"Let's start with the variation Maizie believes, the one she thinks robbed Tom of his reasoning abilities."

Rich opened the freezer section of the refrigerator, took out the old ice and dumped it in the sink. Once that was done, he straddled one of the kitchen chairs. "Basic legend is that the dead sometimes got trapped in the mist and their spirits can't break away from the mountains."

"Why would it trap them?"

"That's the part that varies according to who's telling the story. Some think it's a form of punishment. Some say the undead are warriors left to guard the land. Some believe it was because they had some task that was still unfinished and they can't be released until they fulfill their obligation."

"That's downright creepy." But she could see where they got that idea. The mist had seemed almost alive the other night when she and Rich had hiked to the ravine. "Do they believe all the ghosts are Indians?"

He exhaled slowly, and she got the distinct impression that it bothered him to talk about this. She didn't know why. It wasn't as if she was going to jump on the ghost bandwagon.

"Some folks think that when the original Fernhaven Hotel burned to the ground that a large number of the guests were trapped in the mist."

"Why would they be trapped?"

"I don't know. It's a ghost story. It doesn't have to make sense."

"It could be that when the guests died so suddenly, many of them were in the prime of life," she said.

"Who cares? It's fiction. Get it?"

"Don't patronize me."

"Then make sure you remember that wasn't a ghost who abducted Elora Nicholas and shot Bart. It was a live, human killer that I plan to apprehend."

"That *we* plan to apprehend," she corrected him.

"Whatever." Rich stood and scooted the chair back to the table, clearly ready to drop the conversation.

She wondered if he really feared she was flaky enough to buy into the ghost story if he talked about it too much. If so, he had a lot to learn about her. Not that she gave a darn if he learned it or not. When this case was over, she hoped to be through working with him.

Her mind went back to Bart. God, how she'd love to talk to him about this and get his take on the ghost gambit and how that might or might not hinder their chances of getting the locals to work with them on this.

Bart's insight in situations like this was always amazing. He wasn't from around here, not even from the state of Washington, but he had a way of getting people to open up to him—the way he'd got her to talking about herself that night after she'd first had to pull her gun on a suspect.

She'd spilled her guts, shed a few tears and then ended up laughing over a stale cream-filled donut in the middle of the night.

Rich turned and walked toward the front door with the mixed-breed hound at his heels. He didn't bother telling her he was ready to cut out anymore than he'd asked her if she wanted to stop at his grandparents' house in the first place. He just did things. Maybe it was the mountain way, but she doubted it. It was more likely the Rich way.

She mulled over the ghost idea as she followed him to the car. She didn't buy the legend, but something might have happened that night to spook old Tom right out of his mind.

If so, the investigation could get really creepy before it was all said and done. But in the end, they'd get their man. She had no doubt of that.

Their killer was not trapped in the mist.

KATRINA HELD the diamond-and-emerald pendant in her palm, letting the silver chain loop around her fingers. The jewels warmed her hand as if they contained a literal fire. It was the only warmth she felt anymore, and it made her ache to get on with this and finish what she was here for.

She stood in front of the window, watching the world go by, a world she didn't understand anymore. Maybe she never had. She'd certainly gotten love all wrong. And when love was wrong, all of life was wrong.

She wondered if the man she'd seen in the ballroom the other night had gotten love all wrong? Or was he still searching? She thought it might be the latter. His eyes had been so penetrating, so intense she'd felt as if he were touching her.

She hadn't seen him again, and she hoped she didn't. Of all the nights she might have yearned for his company, now would be the worst time to feel any kind of attraction or form even the most pregnable of bonds.

Still she was aware of him, sensed that he was

here in the hotel. But why? Not for fun. There hadn't been a glimpse of frivolity in his eyes. And here she was thinking of him when all her thoughts should be on the reason she was here.

Katrina left the window and stepped into the hallway. She had to keep her mind clear. Her task was simple, but there could be no mistakes.

She slipped the pendant into her pocket. It was the key to everything.

FOR A HOTEL that had been crawling with security guards ever since the abduction, Bart found it surprisingly easy to move through the building at will. If he'd been officially assigned to the case, he could have never taken such liberties. There were definitely advantages to working a crime detail without the restricting properties of a badge.

He'd already learned a lot, though most of his facts had come from eavesdropping rather than snooping through guest rooms. Jeff Matthews, the young Caucasian in room 211 puzzled him.

Supposedly, he was a freelance travel writer and photographer, but Bart had spotted him following a blond woman the other day at a distance and shooting candid shots of her through a high-powered binocular lens. Bart doubted the shots would ever show up in a travel magazine.

He watched while the photographer stepped out the door of his hotel room, then waited until he was on the elevator before Bart slipped into his room. Breaking in was easy. Locked doors never stopped cops.

As expected, photographs were scattered about the room, spread out on the round table by the window, displayed on the bed and even lined up on the floor.

Bart checked them out. The ones on the bed were of a starlet he'd caught on the late show a few weeks back. One snapshot showed her in the garden, lip-locked with a movie-star handsome guy Bart had spotted getting off the ski shuttle yesterday.

The photos spread on the table seemed more legitimate. They showcased the magnificent foyer, the garden gazebo and the sparkling crystal chandeliers in the ballroom. Looking at the photographs, it was clearer than ever that the whole place was a monument to the past. The photos could have come straight from a 1930s travel magazine.

The photos on the floor were puzzling. They looked like mistakes, but Bart couldn't imagine a professional photographer saving his errors.

He stooped to get a better look. They appeared to be shadows, most dark, but some with an eerie glow to them.

They had been taken on Fernhaven property, inside the hotel, near the more secluded cabins, and some in the wilderness areas.

One grabbed his attention and held it. He picked

it up and studied it. The snapshot was mostly trees and shadows. Yet, it held a frightening familiarity for him. Or maybe it was just that the picture took him back to that horrible night when he'd taken the bullet.

He returned the picture to the floor, leaving it exactly as he'd found it. But as he opened the door and stepped into the hall, he decided that Jeff Matthews was worth watching. He might be a photographer just as he claimed, but he could be more. He could be a murderer.

But then so could dozens of the other men who worked or were registered at the Fernhaven Hotel.

Bart was almost to the stairwell when he sensed someone following him. He spun around to find the old woman he'd met in the garden the other day just a few steps behind him.

"You get around," she said.

"You, too."

"Not so much. Mostly I stay in the garden."

"Then I'm surprised you're not there now. It's a beautiful day for mid-December and it may be the last we have for awhile. They're predicting snow in the mountains by the end of the week."

"Snow can be beautiful, or deadly." She shuffled forward and laid a hand on his arm. "She's in the garden, just past the fountain where I was when we last talked."

The woman's change of subject confused him for a second. "Are you talking about Katrina?"

"Yes. If you hurry, you can find her."

"Did you look for me just to tell me that?"

"It's not as if I have a lot of other things to do."

"Does she know you came to find me?"

The old woman smiled sheepishly, her wrinkled lips almost disappearing as she did. "If she knew, she'd leave before you got there."

"You're not trying to play matchmaker, are you?"

"What if I am?"

"You'll be disappointed. I'm not exactly what you'd call a great catch."

"But you might be exactly right for Katrina. You'll never know unless you give it a try."

He knew, but still he wanted to see her again. "Thanks for the information."

"Just don't disappoint her."

"I'll try not to." That was as much as he could promise. He didn't know if he'd disappoint her or not since he had no idea what she'd want from him—if anything.

He gave the woman a parting smile and hurried away, taking the stairs two at a time, as he'd always done. He didn't know what he'd say to Katrina if he found her in the garden. He'd never been good at small talk unless it involved crime, and there was no reason to suspect she'd be interested in police work.

He raced through the hotel and took the double

doors to the garden. It was nearly deserted, but he passed a woman pushing her baby in an old-fashioned perambulator and a man sitting in his wheelchair reading. Neither of them made eye contact as he walked by.

Katrina wasn't near the fountain and neither was anyone else. He was about to give up when he spotted her standing in a cluster of potted tree peonies obviously straight from the hotel greenhouse.

She looked even more beautiful than the silky blossoms, and he stood there and stared like some awkward teenager. She was dressed differently than she'd been the first time he'd seen her. The dress was not as formal, not as revealing. She looked younger, more innocent. The dazzling pendant was missing from her neck, but her eyes sparkled as brightly as the diamonds had.

No two ways about it. She got to him. He should turn around and walk away. Forget that. She was moving toward him, her full lips slightly parted, her red skirt dancing just above her shapely ankles.

"Are you looking for me?"

Her bluntness surprised him, especially when he'd expected she'd ignore him. "Yes," he answered, thinking even his voice sounded strained since he'd taken the bullet.

"What do you want?"

He tried to think of something clever, or even accurate. Nothing came to mind. "I saw you a few nights ago in the ballroom."

"I know."

"I'd like to get to know you better."

A troubled look settled in her green eyes. "It wouldn't work."

"I'm not trying to make something work. I just thought we could talk."

"About what?"

He had no idea. But now that he was with her, he didn't want to walk away. "Who are you?" he asked.

"Katrina."

"Your last name?"

"It doesn't matter."

"Are you married?"

She looked away. When she turned to him again, her eyes were moist.

"No. I was, but no longer."

"I'm sorry."

"So am I." She took a step toward him. "I'm not what you think."

"I think you're beautiful and that I'd like to know more about you."

"Thanks. I'll consider your proposition."

He shrugged. A little conversation didn't actually qualify as a proposition in his book. Besides, he'd never been one to chase a woman who wasn't interested. He wouldn't start now.

"Just forget it," he said. "I thought we might keep each other company for a while, but it's no big deal."

She bent down and picked one of the blossoms, then cradled it in her hand. With little left to say, he started to turn away.

Before he could, she walked toward him, took his right hand and pressed the flower into it. The petals fell apart and caught on the wind, flying around him like drunken butterflies. He caught one between his thumb and forefinger.

"I don't want to forget it. I'd like to see you again," she whispered. "But don't look for me. I'll find you when the time is right."

He felt lighter than air when she walked away and disappeared behind the clusters of potted blooms. He'd never met a woman who intrigued him the way Katrina did. Tough that it had to happen now when he had his work cut out for him.

Timing was everything. Ask any cop who'd ever lived and they'd tell you that.

BY ONE THAT AFTERNOON, Rich and Carrie had made five calls on people from his list and stopped for sandwiches and coffee at a hole-in-the-wall restaurant in Cedar Cove. They'd discovered absolutely nothing new and Carrie was fighting the urge to taunt "I told you so," by the time they pulled up in front of the small white house where Selma Billings lived with her husband Owen and at least three large dogs who looked as if they might think the deputies were their afternoon snack.

Even Rich stayed in the car until a man in overalls ambled out from the far side of the house and called off the barking animals. Still wary, Carrie remained inside the vehicle until it was clear the dogs weren't going to fly into attack mode.

"Morning, Owen," Rich said.

Owen yanked a red mechanic's towel from his back pocket and wiped his hands before extending his right hand to Rich. "What brings you out here? Not more trouble at the hotel, I hope."

"Not that I know of."

"Good. Selma took it hard when that girl was abducted and killed. She's been having a hard time anyway since she lost the baby. She miscarried, you know?"

"I didn't know," Rich said, "but I can see how that would be upsetting."

"Yeah, good thing construction work is slow this time of the year. I've mostly been doing mechanic work around here. If you know anyone who needs their car worked on, send him to me. I can use the money what with Selma's doctor bills and all."

"I guess it's nice that you're a man of many talents."

"It helps," Owen agreed. "Have you got a suspect yet?"

"Not yet, but we're working on it. That's why

we're here. This is Deputy Fransen," he said, motioning toward her. "We'd like to ask you and Selma a few questions. It won't take long."

Owen turned to Carrie, nodded, then turned his attention back to Rich. "If I knew anything, I'd have called you."

"Sometimes a man sees or hears something he doesn't know is relevant, things that only add up when linked with the rest of the evidence."

"I haven't seen or heard anything about that night except what's been in the papers and what folks around here are speculating. But I'll talk to you long as you like. I just don't want Selma dragged into this. She's upset enough as it is. You understand, don't you?"

He looked to Carrie as he made that last statement, as if he expected her to back him up. She did understand, but that didn't change things. "We really need to talk to both of you," she said.

He rubbed a work-scarred hand across his jaw, then shook his head. "She's not in good shape, not good at all. She's back on those pills Dr. George prescribed."

"What kind of pills?" Carrie asked.

"They're supposed to make her less depressed, but they don't seem to be helping much. Besides, there's nothing she can tell you. She hardly leaves the house anymore except to go to the grocery store or over to her mother's."

"Okay," Rich said. "We'll leave Selma out of this. We're just trying to find something to help us get a handle on who might have committed the crime."

"Hope I can help then. The guy needs to be locked away, whoever he is. Locked away or given a taste of his own medicine. Come on back to the garage. We can talk there. It's warmer than standing out in this wind."

Carrie wanted to protest. It wasn't that she was insensitive to Carrie's condition, but Maizie had said ask Selma about the mountains, and that was what Carrie had hoped to do.

Not that she was chasing ghost stories, but what seemed ghostly in the cold mists of twilight might have a perfectly logical explanation. What seemed to be a spirit could well be a living, breathing killer.

They were already following Owen to the garage when the front door of the house opened and a tall, thin woman dressed in jeans and a gray sweatshirt stepped onto the porch. Her long blond hair hung limply past her shoulders and her bangs reached her eyelashes.

"It's okay, baby," Owen called to her. "The deputies are just here to talk. We won't bother you. Stay inside where it's warm."

"You can talk inside," she said. "I don't mind."

"That's okay. We'll use the garage."

"I'll bring out some coffee," she said.

"No, don't bother, baby. They won't be here long." He picked up his pace.

Carrie slowed, then turned back to the house. Selma was still standing there staring at them. She looked like a lost child. No wonder Owen felt he should protect her. Even the dogs had gone back to quietly sit at her feet as if they knew her emotions were fragile.

Selma hugged herself as if to ward off the wind's chill, but she didn't go back inside. She looked right at Carrie, and Carrie had the crazy feeling that she didn't want her to walk away. Maybe she needed someone besides Owen to talk to.

"Your wife looks upset," Carrie said, running to catch up with the men. "Maybe I should sit inside with her while you two talk."

Rich glared at her. She ignored him.

"I won't question her, Owen. I won't talk at all unless she brings up something she wants to talk about."

He pulled his lips taut and rubbed his chin again as if her offer required some major thought. "That might be good," he said. "She could probably use some woman company. Just don't upset her."

"I won't ask any questions about the abduction."

"You're sure?"

"Absolutely."

"Then I guess it would be all right. She's not well. Even if she talks, it won't make sense."

That was it—way easier than she'd imagined. Rich was still glaring, no doubt sure she wasn't going to keep her promise. That's how little he knew of her.

Carrie hurried to the house. And for the millionth time in the past few weeks, she wished Bart was here. He'd know just how to handle this.

Selma was still standing at the top of the steps when Carrie reached them. She didn't even ask why Carrie had come back. She just walked to the door and opened it, as if she'd been expecting Carrie's company all along.

Chapter Four

The first thing that struck Carrie when she was close enough to really see Selma was how fragile she looked. The second was her age. She'd guessed Owen to be in his mid-forties and expected Selma to be the same.

Now she thought she might be as young as thirty, though it was difficult to tell. Her eyes were puffy and ringed in dark circles as if she'd been ill or wasn't getting enough sleep.

"Can I get you something?" Selma asked. "I have coffee, or a soft drink?"

"A glass of water would be nice."

"I'll be right back."

Carrie looked around, noticing everything the way she'd been trained to do. The living room was clean, but small, barely big enough for the flowered sofa and worn recliner that faced what looked to be a new, wide-screen TV. There was a bouquet of silk flowers on the coffee table and a basket of magazines and newspapers next to the recliner.

A small metal bookshelf next to the TV held a selection of movies, a Bible and a couple of framed photographs. Carrie walked over and had just picked up one of the pictures when Selma rejoined her.

"That's Owen and I the day we got married."

Carrie looked closer, amazed to find that the neatly dressed and well-groomed man in the photo actually was Owen. He was wearing a pair of blue slacks and a white shirt with a tie. Cleaned up, he wasn't half-bad.

Selma was in a pale pink dress with a rounded neckline, a fitted waist and full skirt. She was smiling in the picture, and there were no dark circles around her eyes.

"You were a beautiful bride."

"Thank you."

"How long have you been married?"

"Four years. We got married as soon as I graduated high school. Mom said I had to wait until then."

So she was only twenty-two. Something had sucked her youth right out of her.

Selma handed Carrie her water, then went to stand by the window that overlooked her small yard and the mountains beyond. There were no other houses in sight.

"Did Owen ask you to come in and sit with me?" Selma asked in an emotionless voice.

"No, I just thought you might like some company."

"He worries about me."

"Why would he?"

"I've... I'm not myself. That's how he puts it, how my family puts it, too." Now her voice sounded strained, and she'd caught a lock of her hair between her thumb and forefinger and was rubbing it as if removing a stubborn stain. "You're here about that woman that was taken from the hotel, aren't you?"

It wouldn't actually be breaking the bargain she'd made with Owen to answer. She'd only promised not to ask questions.

"We're trying to find the man who killed her."

For the first time Selma looked directly at Carrie. "Why would you come to see us?"

"It's just a routine visit," Carrie assured her quickly. "We're talking to everyone who lives in the area, just to see if they've heard or seen anything that might lead us to the perpetrator."

Finally Selma left the window and perched on the edge of a wooden rocker. "You'll never find him," she said.

"Never find who?"

"The man who abducted and murdered that woman."

Carrie leaned in closer. "You talk as if you know who he is."

Selma clasped her hands in her lap. "No, I don't know him."

She knew she'd promised Owen not to ask questions, but there was no way she could let Selma's previous statement go unchallenged.

"Why do you say we'll never catch him?"

"Because he's..." Selma slapped her hand over her mouth as if to silence words she had no control over.

"Because he's what?"

"I don't know."

She started rocking, back and forth, staring into space.

Selma's hold on reality seemed so tenuous that Carrie feared it might snap altogether. Was that what had happened to Tom? Had they experienced something so terrifying in the mountains that it literally drove them crazy?

Carrie took a deep breath. How would Bart handle this? What would he ask Selma?

When in doubt, always go with your gut instincts.

His words flashed across her mind as if he were standing beside her whispering them in her ear.

The back door creaked open. The noise startled her, but it was only Rich and Owen joining Selma and her in the house. Owen crossed the room and put his hands on his wife's shoulders protectively.

"Are you okay?" he asked.

"I'm fine. Deputy Fransen and I were just talking about the fact that we might get snow for Christmas."

Interesting that she felt she had to lie to her husband about their conversation. Carrie would have to find a way to talk to her when Owen wasn't around. And even then, she had to remember that anything Selma said might just be the meanderings of a haunted mind.

IT WAS LATE afternoon and the chill of night had already crept into the air when Carrie took the wide double doors to the garden. She and Rich had spent the past two hours viewing films from the hotel's surveillance cameras from the day of the abduction.

They'd gone through all the film and found nothing suspicious, but Rich was still at it, reviewing ad nauseam. She sipped on the cup of coffee she'd poured from a huge urn in the lobby and dropped to an ornate iron garden bench. The sweet smell of hothouse flowers and the soothing sound of falling water did little to clear her mind.

Ever since their visit to the Billings's home, snippets of her conversation with Selma had played in her mind. It would be easy to dismiss everything she said on the basis of her mental and emotional condition, but suppose it wasn't just idle ravings. If that were the case, she might be their only link to the killer.

"Lift your chin a half inch higher."

Carrie turned to the right at the sound of the weird request. A tall, very nice-looking guy with light brown hair and a fancy camera was smiling at her.

"I said raise your chin, not turn it," he teased, walking toward her.

"What are you doing?" she asked.

"I was trying to take your picture. You messed up the shot."

"Why are you taking my picture?"

"I liked the contrast. Beautiful cop with a gun on her hip sitting peacefully in a tranquil garden." He slung the camera strap over his shoulder, freeing his hands. He extended the right one to Carrie. "Name's Jeff Matthews."

"I'm Deputy Carrie Fransen," she said, "and I don't like to have my picture taken by strangers."

"We're no longer strangers. We're acquaintances. Go to the bar with me, I'll buy you a drink, and we might even become friends."

"I don't drink on duty."

"So when do you get off duty?"

"And I'm not looking for new friends," she added.

"Then I guess I won't ever get to show you the great photos I snapped of you while you were deep in thought."

"I could confiscate the camera," she said.

"Why don't you just pat me down, and we'll call it even."

His light brown eyes danced when he smiled,

and his lips crinkled just right, lending a mischievous air to the masculine lines of his face. She might have been a bit premature in turning down his offer of friendship, but she wasn't ready to deal with anything that even hinted at a romantic relationship right now.

She might, however, be interested in his photos. "Do you work for the hotel?"

"No. I'm freelance. I write and photograph, mostly for travel magazines, but I'll sell to anyone who's willing to pay. The Fernhaven Hotel is the new in-place for rich Americans and European and Asian jet-setters."

"I don't want my picture turning up in a travel magazine."

"Nor would the hotel. They'd be afraid a picture of a sheriff's deputy would remind readers of Elora Nicholas's abduction. Besides, I never include a picture of a guest without their permission. You never know who is vacationing with a party other than their own wife or husband. Travel magazines don't like lawsuits."

"Do you have many pictures of the guests?"

"Quite a few."

"What about the hotel employees? Do you have candid shots of them as well?"

"A few. Why? Don't tell me you think we have a criminal among us—other than the Washington politicians who seem to swarm here on the weekends?"

"I hope not." But it was a definite possibility. "I'd like to take a look at your photos."

"Come by my room, and I'll show you what I have. I'm always glad to cooperate with pretty deputies."

"When's a good time?"

"Now works for me," he said, flashing her another of his sexy smiles.

"Good. I'll just need to let my partner know where I am. He may want to join us."

"*He.* You are a party pooper. But it's room 211. Near the elevator."

Two doors down from the room Elora had shared with her husband. They walked to the patio and reached the double doors into the hotel at the same time as Rich. He grabbed her arm and pulled her aside. "Something's turned up."

"Like what?"

"Our first halfway decent lead."

"From the films?" she asked doubtfully.

"No. I got a call from Stella at headquarters. One of the fingerprints from the last batch came back positive. Turns out one of the hotel employees has a prison record."

"What was the crime?"

"Sexual molestation of his neighbor's three daughters, all minors."

She cringed. "The sick bastard. What's he doing here?"

"Baking, a skill he picked up in a Kansas penitentiary. I'm sure his culinary diploma is as fake as the name and other info he put on his application."

"Is he here now?"

"No. This is his day off."

"Do you know where he lives?"

"One of the cooks gave me directions, said it's about twenty minutes from here. I figure if we leave now, we can make it in fifteen."

"Let's shoot for fourteen," she said, already looking around for the photographer, just to let him know she couldn't look at the pictures now. He'd disappeared, probably already in his room, practicing his pickup lines.

She followed Rich back inside, gearing up for the interrogation while trying not to become too optimistic. But it was great to finally have a lead.

KATRINA WATCHED Carrie walk away with the other uniformed law officer. She'd been watching her ever since she'd come into the garden, trying to familiarize herself with everything about the young woman.

It didn't surprise her that Carrie was beautiful. She'd expected that, but Katrina had trouble getting past the fact that she carried a gun. It didn't seem right, and Katrina had no idea what effect that would have on what she had to do.

It was the first time she'd ever done anything like this, though she'd known the day would come for a long, long time. She'd thought she was ready. Now she wasn't sure.

It wasn't the pendant that worried her. She knew its powers—and its limitations. It was Katrina's own shortcomings that worried her. She'd have to use every option at her disposal to make sure she successfully finished what she was here to do.

And she couldn't let anything get in her way, certainly not the man who had captured her with his gaze the other night and who had come looking for her in the garden. She didn't know his name. It was probably better that way, and yet she found herself looking for him every time she stepped into the garden and listening for the sound of his voice in the hotel's long hallways.

She would like to see him again, but she wasn't sure how much longer she'd be here. Once her task was completed, she'd move on. That was the way it worked. Feelings and desires meant nothing. She was dead to them, at least she should be.

The wide double doors to the hotel opened. A young couple walked out hand and hand, and music drifted into the garden. He took her in his arms on the stone patio and held her close, gazing into her eyes before he took her mouth with his.

And the desires that Katrina wasn't supposed to feel became a raw ache that all but tore her apart.

SELMA STOOD in the narrow kitchen, stirring the pot of stew she'd thrown together after the two deputies had left. She knew their visit would upset Owen, and when he got upset, she could count on a miserable evening. And he was most always upset these days.

She should never have told him about that afternoon in the mountains. Not that she could have kept it a secret. She'd been in such a state of shock, it had taken her hours to find her way back home. Her shirt had been torn open, her jeans ripped from the brush she'd staggered through. And there were the bruises.

Owen padded into the kitchen in his bare feet in spite of the cold. His hair was wet from the shower and all he wore was a towel knotted at his waist. The fluffy, jade-green towels had been a wedding present from her sister Louella. Now Louella would barely talk to her. Like Owen, Louella thought Selma had brought the situation on herself.

And maybe she had.

"I made stew," she said, turning back to watch Owen pull a glass from the shelf next to the sink. "I put in lots of onions, the way you like it."

"I'm eating in town tonight."

"If you're upset about the deputies' visit, you needn't be. They were just here on a routine call. Deputy Fransen said so." It was the first time either of them had mentioned the visit since the deputies had left. Usually it was better not to talk about things that upset Owen, but he was already upset, so it didn't matter much what she said.

"What did you and the woman deputy talk about?"

"Just the weather, like I told you."

"You're sure you didn't mention what you did that day in the mountains."

Her insides started to shake, and she felt as if she were going to pass out. She grabbed hold of the counter for support. "I didn't do anything, Owen. I've told you that over and over. I didn't do anything."

He didn't believe her. He never had. She was such a horrible liar. A horrible person. That's why it had happened and why she'd lost the baby. It was all her fault. "Please don't go and leave me alone tonight, Owen. Please don't."

He glared at her for a few seconds, then turned and walked away. She followed him into the bedroom and watched while he got dressed in the only good slacks he owned, the pair he'd worn the day they were married in the little chapel in Cedar Cove.

He took a blue shirt from the closet, one she'd starched and ironed that morning. He buttoned it, then put on his socks and Sunday shoes.

"Where will you go?" She always asked. He never said, but she knew it was to some other woman, someone he didn't think was tainted. She knew he still loved her. At times he could be so tender. He took her to the doctor to get her medicine. He'd taken care of her after the miscarriage and held her head when she was so sick that nothing would stay on her stomach.

But he hadn't made love to her. Not once since that evening when she'd come down from the mountains in tears.

"Don't wait up for me. I'll be late," he said, picking up his jacket and poking his arms through the sleeves.

Owen had changed since that day in the mountains, but he was still a good man. She'd hurt him, hurt him bad. And even he didn't know the full truth. It would kill him if he did.

That's why she'd have to live with the horrible secret until she died. Sometimes she thought that day couldn't come soon enough.

THERE WAS SOMETHING strange going on at the Fernhaven Hotel. Bart still didn't have a good handle on the situation, but there was too much whispering and too many frightened looks exchanged between the housekeeping crew to believe things were running smoothly.

He did know that one of the maids had been fired that afternoon for allegedly going through one of the guest's belongings. The guest had claimed that her clothes had been moved around in the closet and that at least one of her ball gowns had been taken from the hanger and rehung carelessly. The supposition was that the employee had worn or at least tried on the garment.

At least that was what Bart had gotten from talk in the hotel's laundry room. He didn't have access to the kind of surveillance equipment he'd have had if he'd been on duty officially, but a good cop always found his way around that.

Bart had made friends with one of the third-floor maids right after he'd taken up residence and she kept him informed of all the gossip. She was strange herself, had old-fashioned values and a quaint way of talking that fascinated him.

Most important, she could be trusted not to let anyone else on staff know that he was a cop with a vested interest in the ongoing criminal investigation that the hotel management was trying to keep quiet.

But he had a feeling she wanted something from him. He hadn't figured out exactly what yet, and he didn't have time to give it a lot of thought. Solving his own mystery was the main focus of everything he did—at least it was when Katrina didn't haunt his mind.

He walked down the wide first-floor halls, past the restrooms and a row of conference rooms to the library down by the west stairwell. He'd discovered the library on the first day, but hadn't been back since. Libraries had made him nervous even as a kid.

All that whispering as if talk were going to scare the books off the shelves.

But he'd overheard two of the maids whispering about a book in the library on the history of the original hotel, the one that had been destroyed by the deadliest fire northern Washington had ever seen. Evidently it was the first time they'd ever heard of the tragedy. They were freaked out big time to be working in a spot where so many people had died.

In Bart's mind, they should have been a lot more worried that they might have a killer working alongside them. The dead were the least of their worries. He didn't waste his time pointing that out to them.

The library was stuffy, elegant and deserted. The walls were dark and lined with bookshelves. The rest of the room consisted of clusters of sofas and upholstered chairs, similar to those in the sitting areas in the massive lobby, except that in this light the dark wood seemed almost black.

The local interest books were on the most prominent bookshelves. One on local fauna. One on local flora. One on Indian lore. And a large bound book titled *Ferhanven, Its Promise and Its Downfall*.

He picked up the heavy volume and took it to one of the chairs. He skimmed the first pages, all about the dream of the man and wife who'd first conceived the idea for building the lavish hotel at what he referred to as the crowning point of the Cascades, where the sky and the earth met in an explosion of light and beauty.

No mention of the damp mist that blanketed the area every evening and morning or the wind that could cut right to the bone. But when the sun finally broke through, the skies here were as blue as he'd ever seen them. Not that he'd ever seen that much blue sky growing up in L.A.

He kept skimming, past the details on the construction, stopping at the chapter on the grand opening. He studied the pictures, then leafed through the rest of the book to the last chapter. *The Band Plays as Tragedy Strikes.*

He'd always thought of the 1930s as a time of depression when the county was in bread lines. But obviously even then, there had been a core of the elite who managed to live the good life. The men were in suits and ties, the woman in bright-colored dresses that swept the floor, their ears and necks dripping with diamonds and jewels, just as they were every night now in the Glacier Ballroom.

He started to close the book. That's when he saw her. The green satin dress. The red curls framing her beautiful face. The pendant. One magnificent emerald surrounded by flawless pale yellow diamonds.

His Katrina in a picture taken over seventy years ago.

Chapter Five

The mountain road narrowed even more once it passed the turnoff for Fernhaven. The climb was steeper, and the curves were sharper with treacherous cliffs on the right. Carrie was thankful Rich was doing the driving and that they'd only passed one car and two motorbikes so far.

"Strange place for an ex-con from Kansas to end up," Rich said.

"Did the records show any family here?"

"Didn't show any family at all," Rich said. "He's an only child of a single parent, Janie Grant. His name is Harlan Grant, though he calls himself Jason Peters now. His mother died of cancer while he was doing time."

The taillights of a vehicle came into view, the first one they'd seen going north. Rich slowed accordingly. There would be no passing on this road.

"If he was guilty as charged, he's scum," Rich said. "If he's our perp, he's just run out of luck."

"No telling how he's going to react to our little surprise visit," Carrie said. "He might come out shooting."

"He could. Hopefully, he'll just think he's part of the routine questioning we've been conducting. Watch everything you say. Don't do anything to tip him off that we know who he is. We don't want him to run before we can get a warrant."

"Give me a little credit, will you?"

"I'm just making sure we're on the same page."

"By giving orders instead of discussing."

"You need to get used to the fact that I don't work like Bart."

"I didn't mention Bart."

"You don't have to. Everyone knows how you felt about him."

"I don't know what you mean. We were partners. That's all."

"Sure. Let's just drop the subject."

Gladly, but that made her no less angry that he'd brought it up. She wasn't about to explain their relationship to him. Not that she could have even if she'd wanted to. She was still trying to understand it herself, or at least deal with it.

"How much farther?" she asked, when the truck in front of them slowed even more.

"We're looking for Leary Road. According to my directions we should be there just about now. The sign's too rattled with bullet holes to read, but supposedly we'll see the remains of a fireplace off to the left."

"I don't know how you expect to see a pile of bricks in the dark."

Turned out it wasn't a problem. Almost before she got the words out of her mouth, the pickup truck they were following turned off, and the headlights fanned across the bullet-riddled sign and a tree-high pile of bricks.

Rich took the turn, then threw on his brakes as the truck jerked to a stop in the middle of the narrow road.

"Looks like trouble," she said, as the adrenaline surged.

"Be ready for anything."

"I'm way ahead of you."

The man in the pickup truck opened his door and stepped out. "Are you looking for someone?"

"Yeah," Rich answered. "We're looking for Jason Peters. I think he lives around here somewhere."

"I'm Jason Peters. What can I do for you?"

"We just have some routine questions to ask. We're doing that with all the hotel employees, I'm sure you've heard some talk about it."

"I've heard."

There was no sign the man was angry or armed. Rich stepped out of the car and pulled his ID. "Deputy Rich McFarland. And this is Deputy Carrie Fransen."

She'd already stepped from the car and taken out her ID by the time Rich made the introductions. She flashed it as she sized up the man who called himself "Jason Peters." Harlan Grant was average height, a few inches under six feet, weight around a hundred and sixty pounds, average-looking, no visible identifying marks or scars. He was wearing a light jacket with a ski hat pulled low over his forehead that totally hid his hair.

Nothing in his appearance to indicate he'd done time for sexual molestation, yet it was all Carrie could see when she looked at him.

Harlan clapped his gloved hands together, then rocked back on his heels. "Been easier to talk to me at the hotel," Harlan said. "I'm there five days a week."

Rich returned his badge to his pocket. "We don't like to interfere with the workers when they're on duty."

"Whatever. Best if we talk here. My cabin's three more miles down this sorry excuse for a road."

Rich rested his hand on the butt of his gun. "Then why did you stop here?"

"Mine is the only cabin on this road, so I figured you were either lost or looking for me. Hate to ask people to drive this road. Spring thaws tear it up good."

"Still, it must be travelable since you make it to work five days a week."

"Just trying to make it easy on you."

"We appreciate that, but we'll take our chances on the road. It's too cold to talk out here."

Harlan shrugged and walked back to his pickup truck.

Carrie climbed back in the car and buckled her seat belt. "I'd say he definitely doesn't want us at his cabin."

"Or else he's stalling for time," Rich said, revving the motor a few times for good measure.

They easily kept up with Harlan for the first couple of miles, but then he speeded up, driving even faster than he had on the highway.

Rich hit the accelerator. "Looks like our suspect is in a bit of a hurry."

The truck's taillights disappeared, and Rich accelerated again. Carrie glanced at the speedometer just as Rich threw on the brakes. The car skidded a few feet and came to a stop inches from the pickup truck that once again sat in the middle of the road. This time the headlights were out, and the driver's door was open.

"Cover me." Rich pulled his gun, jumped from the car and rushed to the truck.

She jumped out of the car and stooped behind the open door.

"He's gone," Rich yelled back. "Get back in the car and watch his truck. If he comes back, apprehend him. If you have to shoot, aim to kill."

By the time the last words were out of his mouth, he'd already disappeared into the woods in hot pursuit.

Rich was in the thick of the action, and she was left behind. Her own fault. She could have just as easily made the decision and shouted orders at him. Now she was stuck here watching the truck.

Rich was right. This could all be a trick. Harlan might have intended to lure them into a chase through the woods, then he'd circle back and escape.

Gunfire echoed through the mountains. Her blood ran cold. One shot. Just one. But who had pulled the trigger?

The woods became deathly quiet and the waiting became almost unbearable. It was always better to be in the thick of the action.

She scanned the area. How long should she wait before she went into the woods to find out what happened? For all she knew, Rich could be bleeding to death right now. Harlan could have worked his way back to the highway and be looking for a new way to escape.

Ten more seconds. That's all she'd wait. She counted to five before the engine of the pickup truck roared to life and the truck tires spun into action.

The truck hit the shoulder, slinging mud as it flew around her, headed toward the highway. Somehow Harlan had sneaked back into the truck. Unless she stopped him, he was going to get away.

She threw the patrol car into gear and took off after him. She bounced along the road, hitting every pothole, one so deep, her head slammed into the top of the car. And still he was getting away from her.

She pushed the accelerator to the floor. Her back tires hit a slick spot and started spinning. She tried to get the car back on the road, but it was out of control. Her head and shoulder slammed against the door and window.

This was it. The car was careening down a steep hill, maybe the drop-off Harlan had talked about.

And then it slammed to a stop. Something hit her in the face, choking her and squashing her against the seat. If this was what it was like to die, it was totally overrated. There wasn't a bright light in sight and her life didn't march in front of her eyes.

But her shoulder felt as if someone had ripped it from her arm. And her head was pounding.

She searched for the gun she'd dropped when the car left the road. She found it on the seat beside her. Clutching it in her hands, she closed her eyes and fought the pain a few seconds before she radioed headquarters to apprise them of the situation. Her head was spinning so she wasn't sure she made sense.

Damn you, Bart. You should have been here.

And then she just leaned back and gave into the tears she'd kept inside since the night she got the news that Bart had been shot.

BART HEARD the music from the Glacier Ballroom long before he reached its doors. He was arriving early tonight and he'd stay until he saw Katrina or until the music had stopped and there were no dancers whirling beneath the crystal chandeliers.

The woman in the picture looked exactly like Katrina. The red hair piled on top of her head, the eyes, even the pendant. It was as if she'd stepped out of the photograph and into his life.

There had to be a reasonable explanation for this, but for the life of him, he couldn't come up with it.

He slipped through the doors of the ballroom. They were playing "White Christmas" and thousands of glittering pseudo snowflakes danced from invisible wires suspended from the high ceiling. A woman in a blue cocktail dress smiled at him, and her full red lips parted seductively.

He smiled back but kept walking. He had to position himself so that he could see the whole room. He wanted to know the moment Katrina stepped inside. Anticipation was strong, but something else was stirring inside him as well.

It was almost as if someone was calling him. He looked around, half-expecting to see Carrie even though he'd seen her leave the hotel with Rich a good thirty minutes ago.

"Would you like to dance?"

He looked at the woman who was standing

directly in front of him. She was pretty, but she wasn't Katrina.

"I have two left feet."

"You won't if you dance with me. I bring out the best in my partners."

"It sounds tempting, but I'm waiting for someone."

"Just my luck."

"You may know her," he said. "Her name's Katrina."

The woman backed away as if he'd said something offensive. "Do you know her well?"

"No, I only met her a few days ago."

She stepped closer, leaning in until the peaks of her breasts brushed against him. "Katrina moves in circles of danger. If you let her, she'll draw you in."

"What kind..."

The woman didn't wait for him to finish his question before she floated across the floor and found a more cooperative dancing partner.

So Katrina moved in circles of danger. No wonder he found the woman fascinating. To a cop, danger was the biggest turn-on of all.

But that didn't explain her identical appearance and dress to the woman in the picture.

CARRIE PUT HER HANDS over her ears to block the shrill noise that echoed through her brain.

"Looks like you're coming to."

Coming to? Confusion fogged her mind, and she tasted blood. "Will you turn off that damn noise?"

"Can't be hurt too bad if you're that grouchy."

She tried to sit up straight but sank back into the seat as it all came back to her. The gunshot. Chasing the truck. Running off the road. And then she must have passed out. She groaned as a stabbing pain shot through her left shoulder. "You better be shot," she mumbled, "after leaving me alone to chase that lunatic. Oww..." She dissolved into a groan. "Did he get away?"

"Double bad news. I'm not shot, and he got away."

She glanced at the speedometer. They were doing about ten miles an hour. "Do we really need the sirens at this speed?"

"I was hoping someone would stop and offer you a ride to the hospital. At this rate, it will be morning before we get down the mountain."

He turned off the siren. The shrill scream was replaced by clanging and scraping sounds. "I must have banged the car up pretty bad."

"You could say that. The front fender's slapping against the wheel and the hood looks like it was caught in a rock slide. But at least it's running. Otherwise I'd be hoofing it and you'd be lying back there in the ditch."

"You'd leave me back there?"

"Not forever. I'd send someone back for you."

"Gee thanks." Her head was battling it out with her shoulder for agony honors, but she was thinking more clearly. They'd goofed up, and not just with the car. "If the suspect is on the loose, why are we driving back down the mountain?"

"I have an injured partner."

"Not that injured. I just…owwww." She tried to bite back a groan at a new stab of pain, but failed. "I can walk."

"Tell it to the doctor. We're in a dead zone for the cell phone but I called in on the squawk box. The sheriff said take you to Fernhaven. He's sending a doctor and an ambulance."

"Why did you do that?"

"You were knocked out. It's standard procedure."

"What about the suspect?"

"He's sending Kirk to scour the area with me. And he's calling some of the nearby police departments to request some manpower to help in the search."

That was the problem with a small department like they had and a big area to cover. They were stretched thin with routine business. When an emergency came up, they were pushed to the limits.

This was her fault. She should have kept the car on the road. Now Harlan Grant had slipped right through their eager little hands. "He has to be the man we're looking for," she said, thinking out loud. "He wouldn't have run if he wasn't."

"Running isn't evidence."

"It's a good indicator."

"Damn good, but not foolproof."

"I'm surprised he took the job when he realized they were going to take his fingerprints," she said, wishing her head would quit throbbing.

"He probably figured they'd never run them through the system unless he got into trouble."

"Then abducting a woman on the property wasn't too smart. Obviously the hotel didn't do much of a background check on their employees, either, since Harlan couldn't have any kind of viable background as Jason Peters."

"Or he could have a spotless record," Rich said. "All Harlan had to do was steal and use the real Jason Peters' social security number."

"Another use of identity theft." Carrie found the goose egg on her forehead with her fingertips and gingerly traced the swollen flesh. She might have a concussion. Even if she didn't, she was going to feel like hell tomorrow.

She wondered if things would have gone differently tonight if she'd been with Bart instead of Rich. In all honesty, she doubted it. Bart hadn't fared too well against the guy, either—if in fact this was the perpetrator who'd abducted Elora and put a bullet into him.

A shrewd, cunning, murderous pervert. She was probably lucky to be alive. A lot luckier than Elora.

But if he wasn't apprehended and locked away, he'd strike again. She was as sure of that as she was that the sun would rise in the morning or that the mountains would sleep under a blanket of icy mist.

IT WAS a quarter past nine when Katrina made her way down the heavily polished wood floors to the Glacier Ballroom. Sometimes she came early, but most nights she stayed away until the bewitching hour when the surreal became commonplace and magic danced in the soft shadows of the hotel's walls.

But tonight there was something sinister in the air, much as there had been the night the young woman had been abducted. It frightened her and put added pressure on her to do what she had to do quickly.

And still she hadn't been able to get the man out of her mind. She'd tried to find out his name, tried to find out why he was here and why he stayed to himself. No one knew him. No one but the old woman, and she was always so mysterious it was a waste of time to even try to communicate with her. She only talked clearly when it suited her purpose.

Katrina wondered if the man would come looking for her in the ballroom tonight or if he'd forgotten all about her after their encounter in the garden. He probably thought she was a snob. He couldn't know that it was fear that held her back.

Fear he'd find out her secrets. Fear she'd like him too much and let him complicate things that had to stay simple and direct. Fear he'd get in the way of the one thing she had to be certain went right.

Anxiety surrounded her like a stifling fog as she stepped into the ballroom. She skimmed the room expectantly, knowing she'd be better off if he wasn't there, but still hoping to see him. The band was playing a romantic ballad, and the floor was filled with couples dancing close.

The music stopped and the couples drifted back to their tables. It was easier to see about the room now, but still she felt his presence before she saw him. It was because he was behind her, yet close, at her elbow, in her space.

"Hello, Katrina."

Even his voice affected her. It was deep, male, warm.

"Hello."

He took both her hands in his. "I hoped you'd come tonight."

"I heard the music. It lured me here."

He massaged the backs of her hands with his thumbs. "I was hoping I was the lure."

"I don't know you that well. I hardly know you at all."

"You could. I'm not a mystery, not like you."

She looked away as the band started the next song. It was another slow one. Couples began to push by them as they made their way to the dance floor.

"Would you like to dance?"

She hesitated.

"Just a dance, Katrina. Not a marriage proposal."

"No. I didn't think you meant..." He was teasing. She felt a blush though she wouldn't have thought that possible after all she'd been through. "Okay, but I haven't danced in a long time. I'll be rusty."

"I'll chance it."

He took her right hand and led her the few steps to the dance floor. Once there he fit his hand about her waist and began to sway. A million sensations hit her at once, some familiar, some she was sure she'd never felt before.

She was positively giddy. There was no other word that fit the light-headedness and the feeling that she could do this forever. She couldn't, of course. That's why she had to squeeze every fabulous feeling she could from this moment.

Neither of them said a word until the music stopped. "See, that wasn't so bad," he said as he led her off the floor.

"Not bad at all," she agreed.

The band started again, but this time the music was jumpy and the rhythm seemed disjointed.

"Can't dance to hip-hop," he said, "but I can stand out there and do this while you dance."

He did some crazy moves with his arms and legs, and she laughed out loud. She'd forgotten how great laughing felt.

She linked her hand through his arm. "Why don't we take a walk in the garden instead?"

"Only if you promise not to disappear on me the way you did last time."

The thought had occurred to her. She might be forced to escape later, but not yet. She'd already crossed lines she'd thought impassable. She may as well keep the illusion going awhile longer.

Once they were outside, he took off his suit jacket and draped it around her shoulders.

"You'll freeze," she said.

"No. Cold doesn't bother me."

She wondered what did bother him. She wished she knew everything about him, but she didn't dare ask too many questions. If she did, he'd feel free to ask her things she could never make him understand. She let her arm drop from his.

They walked past a row of perfectly manicured hedges. His hand swung beside hers for a second and then he caught her fingers with his and let them tangle. Like lovers. Like normal people with hopes and dreams.

She couldn't go on like this. She had to tell him. But first she should at least know his name. "What should I call you?"

"Bart Finnegan."

"Bart. I like it. It sounds like the name of an athlete."

"I played a little football in high school."

"So what do you do now?"

"Right now I'm a deputy with the local sheriff's department. But I've done a bit of everything. Military. House painter. L.A. homicide detective."

"What an interesting life."

"It's had its moments. Now let's talk about you."

"I've never really done anything."

"Then let's start with your last name."

"Ah, but then I'd lose my aura of mystery. Better to just think of me as Katrina."

"Will you tell me if I guess it?"

"And then you'll take my firstborn, Rumplestilskin."

"No way. I don't do diapers."

She laughed again, so aware of him, she could barely keep from floating down the flagstone path.

"If you guess right, I'll admit it."

"Okay, let's see. Katrina Smith?"

"Smith. You think I'm plain. Admit it."

"Plain as dirt. Katrina Caruthers?"

"No, but I like the sound of that."

"Then, let me think. Katrina…Katrina… Katrina O'Malley."

She stopped walking. "How did you know?"

"Lucky guess."

"No, it wasn't a guess. How do you know?"

"I saw a photograph of a woman who looked just like you in a book in the hotel library. She died in the first Fernhaven the night it burned to the ground, a victim of the tragedy. Her name was Katrina O'Malley."

"You're a smart man." Still, he didn't have it all figured out. If he had, he wouldn't be here now.

"I'm just good with hunches. So who's the woman in the picture who looks so much like you?"

She should tell him the truth. But if she did, she'd never see him again. And she wanted one more dance before that happened. A few more seconds in his arms. One last taste of what could never be hers.

"She's my great-grandmother."

He looked puzzled. "Really. I'm surprised you came to the hotel knowing she died in the original Fernhaven."

"It's the reason I came. The O'Malley family roots run deep."

"They must if you had a necklace made to match the one she had on the night of the fire." He trailed her neck with his fingers, then let them linger on the diamond-and-emerald amulet. "Or is this the original?"

"Yes." The word was barely a whisper. His face was so close. She couldn't fight this. The attraction was too unexpected and far too overpowering. "It was found and returned to us."

"It's beautiful. You're beautiful."

And then he kissed her. The world began to spin as if she were on a mad carousel. She kissed him back, over and over until every part of her was lost in the passion and need.

A siren sounded in the distance, growing closer and closer. Bart pulled away. "I have to go. Duty calls."

She only nodded. She didn't trust herself to speak.

"Tomorrow night in the ballroom. Same time?"

She nodded again.

His hand trailed her arm one last time, as if he hated to leave her. Once he was gone, she hugged her chest, as if that could hold her together.

Bart Finnegan. She wanted to see him tomorrow night, and the night after, and the night after, and every night for as long as she could. But how long would he stay around once he knew the truth about her?

The answer was simple. He'd leave in a heartbeat.

Chapter Six

Bart took a shortcut, avoiding the ballroom and the interior of the hotel altogether. He reached the circular drive in the front just as Sheriff Powell pulled up in his unmarked car and killed the portable flashing lights and siren.

Something pretty big had to have broken for the sheriff to show up this far out of town at this time of the night. The easiest thing to do would be to rush up to him and ask what the hell was going on. But that would open a ton of complications, and make it impossible for Bart to work behind the scenes the way he was doing now.

Best to hang out of sight, but close enough to see and hear what was going on. That should be easy enough with the sheriff and his booming voice claiming all the attention. Powell ordered the valet to leave his car where it was easy to get to since he wouldn't be here long. Before the sheriff reached the door, Rich McFarland came walking out.

"Is the doctor here yet?"

"He's come and gone," McFarland answered, conveniently walking toward where Bart was located behind a guest's waiting limo. "He tried to get Carrie to go into the hospital for X-rays, but she refused."

"Most hardheaded woman I've ever met," Powell said. "But a damn good deputy. So, where is she?"

"She's resting. Hotel gave her a room for the night."

"They damn sure should have. If they screened their employees appropriately this wouldn't have happened. We'd have known they had a man with a prior sexual molestation conviction working here and already had the guy in for questioning or at least had our eye on him." Powell rubbed his hands together as if to warm them. "What's your take? Is Carrie all right?"

"She's got an impressive goose egg on her left temple, and the doctor says she has a mild concussion. He wants her to rest for a day or two."

"She won't," Powell said.

"She might. She's damn lucky," McFarland said. "You'll see how lucky when you see the car."

Powell groaned. "Guess I can't put that off any longer. Lead me to it."

Bart felt like an outsider, as if he were watching from another dimension. It didn't bother him as much as he'd expected, at least now that he knew Carrie was all right.

He had trouble relating with women. Always had—except for Carrie. They'd hit it off from the day he signed on as deputy and was paired up with her on a murder case. There weren't a lot of murder cases in this part of the state, but some guy out on Kettle Road had killed his wife in a fit of rage over a burned steak.

He'd gone to a lot of trouble to hide his tracks, but in the end, they'd got the evidence for a conviction.

Carrie was so green she could have passed for grass. She'd signed on only a couple of months before him, just out of college with her crisp little degree in law enforcement framed and hanging on the wall in her tiny little office down at the department. But she was a good listener and a fast learner. Cute as a button. Outgoing. Enthusiastic.

Cheerleader with a gun, that's what he'd called her.

He followed the sheriff and Rich to the spot where they'd parked the wrecked vehicle, out of sight of the people staying at the plush hotel. The right front fender was hanging on by a thread of metal and a prayer. The right front wheel was knocked a little cockeyed. The front bumper and grille were smashed in.

Powell let out a low whistle, then choked on the

effort. "You guys will do anything to get a new car." He rested his hand on the mangled fender and stooped to get a better look at the damage. "Hard to believe Carrie walked away from this."

"Thanks to the air bags and a guardian angel or two."

Bart stayed around until he heard the full story of what had happened when they'd gone to question Harlan Grant, alias Jason Peters. If Harlan was the murderer they were after, he might be on the run now. He could be anywhere. That could make what Bart had to do a lot more difficult. But then there was no proof Harlan was the man—or that he was gone.

Either way, the killer could still be in the area, perverted, dangerous. Already searching for his next victim.

Brash enough that he wouldn't hesitate to shoot a cop. And Carrie was putting herself right in the line of fire. She'd survived tonight. Next time she might not be so lucky. One more reason he had to work fast. Any cop worth his badge was there when his partner needed him.

And as far as he was concerned, he was still Carrie's partner and this was still his case. He'd started it. He'd finish it. Department rules be hanged.

IT WAS MIDNIGHT, and Owen still wasn't home. Selma paced the small house, hating the cold that crept under the cracks around the doors and windows and the regret that iced her heart. If she'd gone to see her mother that day or cleaned house or worked in the garden, nothing would have happened.

Owen had warned her that it was dangerous to hike the old trail down to Crater Falls alone. But she'd hiked the paths that snaked through the woods and up and down the mountains all her life. The worst she'd ever expected was a skinned knee from slipping on the trail. Never in all her life would she have ever imagined what happened that day.

She shuddered as the memories crept into her mind and the man's touch seemed to slither along every nerve ending. And suddenly the walls of the house seemed to close in on her. She grabbed her parka from the hook by the back door and ran outside.

The cold slap of the wind did nothing to clear her mind. Instead the images grew more vivid. She could taste and feel and smell the day. It had been bright and cloudless. Crater's River had rushed over the rocks as if it were in a hurry to reach the Pacific.

The area she'd stopped in was verdant with lush growth and the odors of damp earth and blossoms from plants that grew wild in the mountains blended into the kind of aphrodisiac that could only be found on a crisp fall day in the Cascades.

She'd stopped at the edge of the river and perched on a rock partly shaded by a young alder tree. Tempted by the lure of the water, she'd slipped out of her shoes and socks and dipped one toe into it. The cold shocked her so that she fell backward and scratched her hand on the rock as she caught herself to keep from falling.

She still remembered the blood trickling over the pattern the twigs made. She'd been staring at that strange, squiggly line when the wind had gusted and the temperature had seemed to plunge at least ten degrees. She'd reached to grab her shoes and socks she'd tossed behind the rock.

That's when he'd stepped from behind the row of evergreens.

The day had been bright and sunny. Yet when she saw him in her mind's eye, he was always shrouded in a heavy mist. His features were never clear; the sensations were frighteningly vivid.

As they were now.

She slid her hands between her thighs and felt the erotic ache that had become so familiar. Moisture pooled in her panties, and her breath came in tiny, heated, gasps.

She'd been on fire. Exploding with desire. Tasted passion like she'd never known existed. And then it had ended. She'd felt more satisfied and fulfilled than she ever had in her life. It had been more than sex. It had been an ethereal ecstasy beyond anything she'd ever felt before—or since.

The shame of what she'd done hadn't hit until she'd started home.

"What are you doing out here in the cold?"

She jumped and bit back a scream. "Owen. You startled me. I didn't hear you drive up."

"Obviously."

"I'm okay," she whispered. "I just stepped outside to look at the moon and get a breath of fresh air."

"And think about him?"

"No, I wasn't."

He didn't believe her. She could see the distrust in his eyes and the cold, hard jut of his jaw.

He turned and marched back inside without waiting on her or giving any explanation of where he'd been. She followed him, hating herself for feelings she couldn't escape and an experience that had no reasonable explanation.

Either she was suffering from anxiety and depression as the psychiatrist said or she was slowly going stark-raving mad. She was almost sure it was the latter.

KATRINA KNEW Carrie was in the hotel. Her arrival in the wrecked patrol car had created a stir that had spread up and down the long hallways. Katrina even knew what room she was in. The temptation was great to forego all the preliminaries and take care of things tonight.

But as much as she wanted to get this over with,

the risk to rush and make mistakes was too high. She had to play by the established rules. Neither the game nor the game plan were her design, but the consequences of failure would all rest on her shoulders.

Still she was far too restless to sleep. She went back to the ballroom. It was empty now, but the music still seemed to echo from the walls, low and haunting, and if she looked really hard, she could see the reflection of dancers weaving their way about the polished floor. Holding each other, falling in love.

Love.

The word floated around her as if suspended in the air like one of the fake snowflakes. The letters were easily recognizable, but the concept was as foreign as happiness or fulfillment.

Deception. She knew that word well. Betrayal. Heartbreak.

Murder.

Those were the words that defined her. But not love. Love was impossible at this stage of the plan. Love and Bart Finnegan.

And yet she was consumed with him. She lifted her long skirt and twirled about the room, remembering the feel of his arms around her, the thrill of having him hold her close, the sweet, salty taste of his mouth.

It wasn't fair. Temptation shouldn't come now

when it was too late to do anything about it. Desire shouldn't touch her. Life shouldn't matter at all.

Only it did.

TWO DAYS AFTER the car wreck and the debacle of losing the only real suspect they had, Carrie was still stiff and achy. The hematoma on the side of her temple where she'd glanced off the side window before the air bags had inflated had gone down considerably, but the bruises on her shoulder were becoming a work of abstract, psychedelic art. Fortunately, the art was hidden under the long sleeves of her uniform.

But she was sore and still tired from the lack of sleep she'd gotten the night she'd spent in the hotel. Her room had been just over the ballroom and the music had seemed to drift right through the floor.

But she had to get back on the job. A lot of things had changed with the case over the past two days. Powell had released the information about the note to Fernhaven's general manager, though not to the press. The manager had promised the hotel's full cooperation with the investigation and with keeping the note a secret.

And they'd requested that Rich and Carrie check out the facilities for any weakness in their security. It was the first time they'd admitted that it could possibly be lax.

"Are you sure you feel up to this?" Rich asked,

as they parked in front of the hotel about three minutes before their meeting with the head of hotel security.

"We're going to talk. What's there to be up to?"

"You could have taken a couple more days off."

"I could have stayed on the road the other night and shot out Harlan Grant's tires and kept him from escaping. So much for woulda, coulda, shoulda."

He bypassed the valet and parked his car in the lot closest to the main entrance. They were in his personal car, an old gray sedan with over a hundred thousand miles on it and the dents and scratches to prove they'd been difficult ones. The department's budget was too tight to have replacement patrol cars collecting bird droppings and waiting for an accident.

An excursion bus was parked in front of the entrance and Carrie and Rich had to wait for a group of teenagers carrying skis to push out the wide doors before they could enter.

"A great morning for the slopes," Rich said. "But the storm's expected to push in by late afternoon. Blizzard conditions predicted by tomorrow morning."

"Maybe Harlan Grant will get stranded in it and freeze to death," she said.

"The world should be so lucky."

She walked inside, unzipping her parka as she did. "I just wish we had proof he's the man we're looking for. I'd feel a lot better putting all our efforts into finding him if I knew we weren't letting the real perp go free."

"Evidence is definitely leaning his way right now."

"We had him in our hands," she said. "And I let him get away."

"*We* let him get away," Rich corrected.

Now he wanted to be a team player. Go figure. "Do you think Harlan's still in the state of Washington?"

"No way to say. Could be anywhere. There's an APB out on him, but that doesn't mean squat. Some men on the FBI's most wanted list have avoided capture for years."

Carrie led the way, past the desk where clerks were checking in newly arriving guests to the hall where the administrative offices were located. They opened the door marked business offices and stepped into a lavishly appointed reception area. The woman behind the mahogany desk was also lavishly appointed. Carrie was certain Rich appreciated the view.

"May I help you?"

"We have an appointment with Chuck Everly," Rich said, stepping up to the desk.

The receptionist checked an appointment book. "You must be Deputies McFarland and Fransen. Mr.

Everly's expecting you. Follow me, and I'll show you to his office."

They followed. Chuck Everly was at his desk, sitting just in front of a large window with a spectacular view of the wooded area and the beginning of the maze of paths that led to the individual cabins. He also had carpet, potted plants, a couple of upholstered chairs and framed prints of the Cascades on his walls. Nice setup for an assistant manager. It said a lot for Fernhaven's profit margin.

Although Carrie had met Chuck a couple of times and talked to him extensively about the case, this was the first time she'd been to his office. On the previous occasions they'd talked over coffee at a back table in the employee dining room. Rich han't met him at all since Chuck had been out of town on business ever since Rich had been assigned to the case.

He stood when they came in and smiled widely, showing a mouthful of perfect white teeth. He was middle-aged, still in shape and dressed in a suit and the trademark green tie that all the male management team wore.

"Good to see you again, Deputy Fransen, though I wish it were under better circumstances."

"So do I."

"I don't know how we messed up with Jason Peters—or rather Harlan Grant. We screen the background of all our employees."

"Your screen must have a few holes," Rich said, then introduced himself. They took the chairs Chuck offered.

"So exactly where are we with Harlan Grant?" Chuck asked. "Can we assume he's out of the area?"

"I wouldn't advise any assumptions where he's concerned," Rich said.

"Then I'll definitely alert my security staff to be on the lookout for him." He leaned back in his chair. "What else did you want to discuss?"

"I'd like to see a list of any guest complaints," Rich said.

"What are you looking for?"

"At this point we're searching for anything that would help us identify the man who abducted Elora Nicholas from your hotel. Maybe a guest reporting suspicious behavior of an employee or even another guest," Rich added.

"Our files are private."

Carrie cringed. Wrong response. Rich was neither patient nor tactful.

"You goofed up once by hiring Harlan Grant," Rich said. "Let's not complicate things with a bunch of privacy boloney. We're not here to write a gossip column. We're here to keep your guests safe."

Chuck frowned. "Privacy is an important issue with us, but of course the safety of our guests is our number one concern. I just want you to understand that what you read should not be released publicly."

"Not unless it directly relates to our case."

"Then why don't I go through them while you check out the facilities? I'll pull anything that might offer you any valuable information."

"I appreciate the offer, but I think we'll just look through the files ourselves."

"You'll waste a lot of time."

"We work fast. You could have someone bring in a pot of coffee, though. Some of those cinnamon rolls from the coffee shop would be nice, too."

"Whatever you'd like, deputy."

"We appreciate your need for confidentiality," Carrie assured him, trying to diffuse the man's obvious irritation. "I promise you that nothing will go outside this room unless it directly affects our investigation."

"I appreciate that, Deputy Fransen." He smiled at her, and ignored Rich. "I can let you see the files under those conditions, but I think it best that I give you a brief summary of what to expect before you start perusing the files."

Something in his voice made Carrie uneasy. It was as if he was warning them that they'd find something they didn't like.

"I don't know how much you know about the history of the hotel or the area," Chuck said.

"We know the original Fernhaven burned down

over seven decades ago," Carrie said, "and that the current hotel was rebuilt in the same spot to look almost identical to the original."

Chuck nodded. "That's part of the problem."

Rich crossed an ankle over his knee. "Problem as in…?"

"You know how some people are. They get it in their heads the hotel is haunted just because people died on this spot. They start to imagine that they see and hear things."

"What sort of things?"

"Harmless things like music coming from the ballroom late at night. We check it out. The doors are locked, and the room is quiet and empty."

"Is that a frequent complaint?"

"I've heard it several times, maybe a dozen. But you know how it is. One person says they hear something, and everybody else gets in on the act."

"Any other strange complaints?" Rich asked.

"Occasionally guests have mentioned things being moved from place to place, lights going out or coming on, unusual shadows on the wall. The typical things people imagine when they believe a place is haunted."

Carrie took a deep breath. "What time does the band quit playing in the ballroom?"

"The traditional Fernhaven ball is only on Saturday nights. The band plays until one and sometimes two for that."

"What about the other nights?"

"Normally they don't play at all, but during the month of December we have music for dancing from nine until midnight, Tuesday through Saturday. And there's live music in the lounge every night until midnight. I'm sure that's what some of the guests heard."

There was always a reasonable explanation for everything—even at the Fernhaven Hotel.

Ghosts and illusions were only figments of troubled minds.

And the music she'd thought she'd heard coming from the ballroom hadn't come from the hotel's band.

ALTHOUGH SUBTLE, and all but invisible to the unschooled eye, security around the main hotel had been beefed up since Harlan Grant had disappeared. There were two more men on duty today. Bart had picked them out early.

One was dressed in a pair of jeans and a navy blue parka. He'd spent most of the morning outside, hiking the trail that wove in and out among the more isolated rental cabins.

The other man looked as if he'd stepped off the pages of a men's fashion magazine. He had the layered look that Bart usually adopted for Sunday morning. Only Bart's layers consisted of an old

T-shirt, a flannel shirt and a worn denim jacket or Seahawks sweatshirt.

This guy's layers were a white T-shirt, a light blue cotton shirt, opened at the neck, and a v-neck sweater in shades of blues, golds and tawny reds. Few of the guests gave him a second look as they hurried by him and the book he appeared to be reading.

They'd have never noticed the way Bart had that he'd been on the same page all morning. Nor would they have noticed that from his vantage point, the man could see everyone who entered or exited the hotel through the main doors.

Bart had already concluded that the main hotel was relatively safe. The cabins were another story. They'd been designed for guests who wanted more privacy. They got plenty of that. Though they were within walking distance to the main hotel, each one was situated so that it couldn't be seen from any other cabin or any other structure on the property.

They'd have been a much easier target for an abduction than the main building, which made Bart wonder why the perp had taken such risk. The variable that sealed the choice may have been that the cabins were occupied for the most part by couples or families and Elora had been going to her room alone after the argument with her husband.

Had the perp seen them argue and followed her? Or was there more to his selection and timing than that? Random? Or specifically chosen? A spur-of-the-moment crime or had he been watching and waiting for the chance to abduct and kill Elora Nicholas?

If Bart had the answers to those questions, he'd feel a lot better about the situation. As it was, he had to expect the worst—that the choice of victim had been random and that the perp could strike again at any time.

It might have been Harlan Grant, but there wasn't enough evidence to that effect for Bart to let down his guard. He still thought it was someone who knew their way around the hotel. That could include kitchen help if Harlan had made it his business to check out everything.

But it could also be a security guard, a maintenance engineer, someone from housekeeping—or a photographer who roamed the hotel at all hours of the day and night shooting candid shots. There were plenty of possibilities still in the immediate vicinity.

But when Bart walked away, it was Katrina who took over his mind. He hadn't seen her since two nights ago when he'd kissed her in the garden, but she'd never been far from his thoughts. His fascination with her bordered on the obsessive, and that frightened him.

No woman had ever mesmerized him the way Katrina did.

Katrina's lips had been incredibly soft, like cotton candy without the sticky sweetness. And when he'd kissed her, he'd felt as if he were floating on air.

And here he was thinking like some damn frustrated poet. The woman got to him. That was all there was to it. He'd have to be more careful with his feelings. This would be the worst possible time to became entangled with a woman who could lure him away from the task at hand.

But he knew if he got half a chance, he'd kiss her again. And he'd love to keep her company when tonight's blizzard came in. And he had a feeling, almost a premonition that he'd get that chance.

Unless the abductor struck first.

HE STOOD in the shadows of the dining room, unnoticed behind the huge urns and potted ferns. His gaze was fixed on the young deputy. She intrigued him and irritated him at the same time.

He'd seen the look on her face when she'd come out of the office of the assistant manager. She was spooked by the creepy things that went on and the mystique of the rebuilt hotel. But that wouldn't turn her away, it would only make her dig deeper. She'd keep prying until she found out something.

He had to kill again. The urge was eating away at him, so strong he could barely hold food in his stomach anymore. So intense, he dreamed about

Elora Nicholas night after night, waking up in a cold sweat but with his body hard and hungry for more of the same.

He had to kill again. So why not make Deputy Carrie Fransen his next victim? All he needed was opportunity, and one of the sharp knives from the hotel kitchen.

Chapter Seven

Carrie sat in the more informal of the two Fernhaven restaurants, sipping a caramel latte topped with a curl of whipped cream and watching the first flakes of snow fall from the gray sky. They'd finished going through the files a half hour ago, and one word seemed to be stuck in her mind.

Haunted.

It was a strange and chilling word. It conjured up images of ghostly figures in white floating down dark, deserted hallways. Images of old houses draped in spiderwebs and with bats clinging to moldy ceilings and rats scampering across splintered floors.

The Fernahaven Hotel didn't gel with the images. So why had there been so many complaints of cryptic sounds and happenings, unless it was just as Chuck said. People came there knowing the original hotel had been destroyed by fire and then let their imaginations work overtime.

That could be all it was. More than one of her psychology instructors had stressed that the phenomena of people seeing and hearing what they expected to see and hear wrecked havoc on eyewitness testimony. No one ever saw any incident in exactly the same way, and much of what people saw was based on their expectations.

That was the perfect explanation for the complaints, especially since only a small fraction of the guests voiced any concerns that could be considered eerie. Perfect, except Carrie hadn't expected to hear flapper music at four in the morning, yet she'd heard it. Perfect, except that one of the guests who'd had the most bizarre complaint of all had been the renowned psychiatrist, Marjorie Libscomb.

Carrie wrapped both hands around her coffee cup, soaking up the warmth. Just thinking about the statements in Marjorie's file gave her goose bumps. She couldn't wait to talk to her about the claims in person.

Actually, she'd wanted to meet Dr. Lipscomb ever since she'd studied her books and attended one of her lectures at the university. She had been much of the influence for Carrie's putting her unhappy childhood behind her and taking charge of her life. She'd been the primary reason Carrie had gone into law enforcement. It forced her to take control and not let life push her around anymore.

"Hello, Deputy."

She looked up to find Jeff Matthews standing over her, his boyish grin in place. He dropped into the chair next to hers without being invited.

"What brings you out in the storm?"

She wiped her mouth with the green napkin. "A few snowflakes don't qualify as a storm."

"But according to the latest weather report, a serious winter storm is headed our way."

"I plan to be home long before it arrives."

"You could always share my room. Save yourself a drive."

"I'll keep that in mind."

"Are you here alone?"

"No, my partner's around, making a phone call. We're heading down the mountain as soon as he finishes." Which might be another half hour. The man spent more time on the phone than any woman she'd ever met.

"Too bad you're not staying over. It would be a great day for you to check out my photographs. You'll have to do it soon if you're going to see them. I'll only be around a few more days. After that my room shoots back up to the regular rate."

"I'd have thought you stayed free in exchange for favorable press."

"But I don't guarantee favorable press. I just tell it like it is."

"Then why do you have a reduced rate to start with?"

"It's an Internet special that I'm sure they offered before they realized they'd be booked solid for the month of December. Still expensive, but luckily it's a tax write-off."

"So how do you rate the hotel?"

"First class all the way. A great vacation spot for those who can afford the very best."

"Or those who can write it off," she countered.

"Perks of the job, though few of the places I write about are this luxurious. Fernhaven is a throwback to the days when people knew how to vacation."

"Then you have no negatives to report?"

"There are always negatives." He waved off the approaching waitress, letting her know he wasn't interested in ordering.

"What kind of negatives?" Carrie asked, probably a little too eagerly.

"You'll have to check out the articles to discover that. First one comes out in *Elite Travel* next spring. And I've sold short articles to a couple of airline publications."

"I'll be sure to look them up." But she didn't want to wait that long to have her question answered. "I've heard some people say the hotel is haunted. I don't suppose you caught any ghosts on film."

The easy smile faded from his lips and the mischievous gaze grew guarded. "Do you believe in ghosts, Deputy?"

She considered the question. She didn't, and yet…

She was saved from having to answer by Rich's timely appearance. "We have to go," he said, without acknowledging Jeff's presence or venturing too far into the restaurant.

She was used to his brusqueness, but he seemed agitated as well. She stood and grabbed her parka from the back of her chair. "Have you heard an update on the weather?"

"No, but I got a call from Maizie."

"Is something wrong?"

"Tom's missing. Maizie thinks he may have wandered into the wooded area behind the house."

Dread kicked in. This was not the day to get lost in the mountains. By the time she shoved her arms into her coat, Rich was gone.

"Guess I'll have to see the photographs later," she called to Jeff as she raced to catch up with her partner before he drove off without her. The snow was barely falling now, but storms had a way of intensifying fast in the Cascades. If they didn't find Tom soon, they wouldn't find him until after the blizzard. And by then he might be dead.

CARRIE TRIED her cell phone as they left the hotel, but as usual, there was no signal. She used the police radio to report the missing man.

"Don't expect much help," Rich said. "There's no

time to get a search and rescue crew in action before the storm hits. It will just be us and family and neighbors."

"How long has it been since anyone's seen Tom?"

"A little over an hour." Rich leaned forward and wiped the condensation from the inside of the windshield with the back of his sleeve. "Maizie drove into Burlington for supplies. The neighbors were watching out for him, but everyone got busy preparing for the storm."

"So they forgot all about him?"

"You can't blame them. No one expected him to wander off. He hasn't left the property since his stroke."

"He picked a great time to start exploring again," she said. She pictured a frail, sickly man trudging through the snow. "How's he dressed?"

"Last time anyone saw him, he was in the old storage shed behind the house. He was wearing his barn jacket and boots then. He's probably warm enough, at least for now."

"Maizie must be scared to death."

"Sounded that way."

Rich said little else on the drive to Maizie's.

Finally, Rich turned down the road that led past his grandparents' house. "You can stay with Maizie," he said. "She'll need someone to keep her from worrying herself to death."

Carrie's blood pressure shot up. "I'm not a baby-sitter. I'm a deputy, remember? The same as you."

"You don't know the area."

"I'll stick close to you."

"You'll only slow me down. Besides, there's no reason for both of us to fight the ice and snow. You might as well stay close to a fire."

The fire sounded a lot more inviting than tramping through the mountains in a snowstorm, but his attitude galled her too much to let her accept the offer. "I'm sure one of Maizie's neighbors or her daughter or granddaughter will stay with her. I'll go with the search team."

"The search team is me."

"I thought you said the neighbors would help."

"They're up there now, but they'll turn back soon. They're older guys. They don't have the stamina for dealing with the storm, and getting stranded up there won't help Tom."

"If you find him, you may need help getting him down the mountains, especially if he's out of his head or hurt. I'm going with you."

"Suit yourself," he said, giving up the argument a lot more easily than she'd expected. "There's a couple of extra wool sweaters in the trunk. I suggest you put one on when we stop. There are extra socks, too."

Luckily he'd come prepared. All she had were her parka and the hiking boots and ski mask that she'd fortunately thought to rescue from the trunk of the wrecked patrol car before it had been towed into town.

Maizie ran out to meet them the second they parked. Snowflakes stuck to her gray hair and thin eyelashes, making her look like one of those snow figures people put on their mantels at Christmas. But the sculptures couldn't have captured the fear in her eyes.

She grabbed both their hands, but her pleading was directed at Rich. "Find him. Please find him. He's all I've got."

"We'll find him, Maizie. You stay inside and keep warm. Make him some soup. He'll need that to warm up his insides when we bring him home."

Rich sounded positive, but when Carrie looked up at the bleak sky and out to the enormity of the mountains, her heart sank. They could promise, but that didn't mean they'd be able to deliver.

And all of a sudden she knew how Bart must have felt when he realized he couldn't save the abducted woman from her killer. Their job was to save lives. Failing, or even the possibility of failing, was difficult to face.

"Ready to go?" Rich asked, once they'd both changed into warmer boots and donned their gloves.

"Ready as I'll ever be."

"Then let's do it."

The ghosts were forgotten as she trudged after him. Reality was all she could handle.

AN HOUR LATER, Carrie was really glad she'd pulled on the extra layers of clothing. She was cold clear through to the bone, but she tried not to think about it. She needed all her concentration for keeping up with Rich and not slipping on the icy rocks.

The snow fell steadily, covering their footsteps as quickly as they made new ones. She'd lost all sense of direction. All she knew was that they were steadily climbing, and that if she became separated from Rich, she'd never find her way back to Maizie's.

Rich obviously knew that, too. He leaned against a tree from time to time and waited for her to catch up with him. He was doing that now, waiting and calling Tom's name the way he'd done every few yards of the search.

His voice was hoarse from yelling into the wind. This time she took over the task for him, calling Tom's name as loudly as she could and watching her breath vaporize in the frigid air.

There was no answer.

"I don't see how we can possibly find him without a larger search team and helicopters," she said. "There's too much land to cover."

"Are you ready to give up and leave him to freeze to death?"

"I didn't say that."

He exhaled sharply, but his features softened. "Sorry. You didn't deserve that. You're doing great."

"Thanks." Coming from Rich, that was an impressive compliment, the first she'd ever heard come out of his mouth, at least the first that applied to her.

"There's a cave not too far from here. I know he knows where it is because he's the one who showed it to me when I was a snotty-nosed kid. I'm hoping he's holed up there."

"Why do you think he came up here in the first place?"

"I wouldn't even venture a guess, except that he's roamed these mountains all his life."

But other possibilities filled Carrie's mind. What if he hadn't had a stroke the day he'd become disoriented? What if he and Selma had actually seen something in the mountains that had pushed them beyond the edge of reason. What if that something had drawn him back into the storm to destroy his body the way it had destroyed his mind?

Oh, geez. The cold must be numbing her brain. Tom was an old man who'd had a stoke. Selma might be schizophrenic or suffering the repercussions of hallucinatory drugs she'd used in the past or might still be using.

And Marjorie Lipscomb?

"Are you okay?"

Rich was waiting on her again. She was slowing

him down and letting herself get spooked wasn't helping her move any faster.

"I'm fine." She sucked in a deep breath and the cold stung her lungs.

Rich called Tom's name again. It caught on the wind and echoed through the mountains. She froze at the sound of a low moan almost lost in the echo. "Did you hear that?"

He rushed toward the sound and she tried to keep up. Her foot slipped on an icy rock and she had to grab hold of a tree trunk to keep from falling. When she looked up Rich had disappeared from sight.

Darn it. She hadn't kept up and now all she could see was endless trees, rocks and snow. And she wasn't about to call out yet and admit she was lost.

She darted a few feet in one direction, then retraced her steps and went in the other. And then she saw Rich. He was hunched over a man who was sprawled out as if he'd been making snow angels.

Rich turned back to her. "I think he's had another stroke, or a heart attack."

"Oh, no." Carrie hunched down beside Rich, then checked Tom's pulse to be certain he was alive. He certainly didn't look it.

When she touched him, he opened his eyes for a second and seemed to be staring at her. "She's got no face."

She thought he was talking about her, and she yanked off her ski mask so he could see her features.

"I don't think he means you," Rich said. "I'm not even sure he realizes we're here. He's talking out of his head."

"He looked right at me."

"He looked at me, too," Rich said, "but he called me by his son's name and Harry's been dead for six years."

"His pulse is weak," she said. "We have to get to a doctor."

"First we have to get him down the mountain," Rich reminded her.

It was going to be a formidable task. He'd be too heavy to carry, and he couldn't possibly walk.

Tom grabbed Rich's hand. "I tried, but I couln't help her."

"That's okay. I'll help her for you." Rich tore off his ski mask and slipped it over Tom's head. "We're going to take you home, Tom. You can sit by the fire with Maizie and then you can tell me all about it."

He mumbled something else, but this time his voice was so low Carrie couldn't make out what he was saying.

Rich pulled up the collar on his jacket, covering his face with it as best he could, then he picked up Tom and threw him over his shoulder like a sack of potatoes—a very heavy sack of potatoes.

"You can't carry him all the way," she said.

"You got a better idea?"

She did, but she hated to say it. "I'll stay with him while you go for help." Stay here in the snow with a seriously sick man mumbling about a woman without a face. She'd surely lost her mind to suggest it, but what else could she do?

"You'd do that?"

She gritted her teeth. "Sure."

"You might make a decent partner after all." But he didn't put Tom down. He started walking, slower now that he was carrying a load.

"I meant what I said. I'll stay with him while you go for help."

"That's real spunk, Carrie. But there's no way I'd let you do that. Either we go down together, or we ride it out together." He kept walking.

The wind picked up, blowing the snow into Carrie's eyes and mouth and making it impossible to see more than a few feet in front of them as they plowed their way toward Maizie's.

She shivered, but not from the cold. Crazy, but she had the weirdest feeling that someone was watching them. She knew it was impossible, but this time she easily kept up with Rich. She couldn't wait to get off the mountain, couldn't wait to go home.

CARRIE MADE IT off the mountain. She didn't make it home. By the time they got to Maizie's and got

Tom to the small county hospital just east of Cedar Cove, the roads to town were impassable.

Now Carrie was toasting by a blazing fire that Rich had built in the stone fireplace that dominated the front room of his grandparents' house. He was a few steps away, in the small kitchen, putting together a pot of chili from ingredients he'd found in Maizie's well-stocked cupboard and freezer.

For the first time since they'd come in from the storm, Carrie actually felt warm, at least on the outside. Her insides were still shaky, her mind cluttered with befuddling thoughts that she refused to deal with anymore tonight.

It was bad enough that she was stranded in a small mountain cottage with Rich McFarland. That in itself could freak a woman out. But she wasn't going anywhere before morning, so she might as well make the most of it.

On the up side, Rich had so far gone out of his way to be hospitable. Apparently being host brought out the best in him. And the odors coming from the kitchen were causing her mouth to water and her stomach to growl now and then in anticipation.

She stretched her feet in front of the fire and wiggled her toes inside the red socks Rich had confiscated for her from his grandmother's bureau. She was wearing one of his grandmother's chenille robes as well. She looked like an unmade bed in it, but it was warm and dry and the only thing in his grandmother's closet that didn't just slide off her when she pulled it on.

Rich, on the other hand, looked damn good. He had a few changes of clothes at the house. Guy must have been a Boy Scout at one time in his life. He was definitely prepared for anything. Probably carried his toothbrush in his pocket and a pack of condoms in his wallet, just in case he got lucky one night.

This wouldn't be the night.

Not that she could even imagine Rich putting the make on her. Hard to come on to a woman without making small talk. She was pretty sure the guy didn't have a clue how to do that.

She stretched to a standing position and walked over to the bookshelves. She scanned the titles. Some classics. A few bestsellers. A couple of poetry collections. And volume after volume of nonfiction books, mostly history, but a few on the Cascade mountains.

Her gaze fastened on one of those. *Mountain Myths and the Paranormal.* She picked up the trade-size paperback and read the tag line.

True tales of the supernatural from those who lived to tell them.

A chill slithered down her spine as she took the book back to her fireside chair and opened it to the first page. The lights blinked, but she barely noticed. The first line had carried her into the ghostly world of the undead.

THE POWER had gone out an hour ago, leaving the hotel guests to dress for dinner by candlelight and the dim glow of the generator-powered emergency lights. There was an air of excitement in the air, as if the storm and the loss of electricity were reason for a celebration.

The mood surprised Katrina. She'd never liked storms. By their very nature, they were unpredictable. They held the power to destroy anything in their paths, just as a fire did when it blazed out of control.

She pushed through the wide doors to the Glacier Ballroom. It was quiet tonight. Even if a band had been scheduled to play, they wouldn't have been able to get to the hotel in the storm. She made her way across the floor in the darkness, not stopping until she reached the glass doors that led to the stone patio and beyond that the gardens.

Snow covered the grounds and new flurries danced in the halo of gas lanterns. The lanterns were a new addition to the landscape, a way to light the pathways leading to the individual cabins when the power was out. She wondered if any of those guests would brave the weather tonight or if they'd order room service and let the hotel crew fight the elements.

As for her, she was glad to be inside the beautiful hotel. But she wouldn't be for long. Her time was running out and her chance of success was becoming more uncertain by the day. What frightened her most was that she might have missed her best chance the other night when Carrie had slept in the hotel.

But the timing hadn't been right. Things weren't in place. And now, she wasn't even sure she could do this without help. She needed someone Carrie would listen to and trust, someone whose orders she'd follow without having her suspicions aroused.

Katrina's concentration intensified. She hadn't heard footsteps behind her, but she knew that Bart had just joined her in the dark ballroom. His essence was as strong as the storm, invading her senses.

He walked up behind her and slipped his arms around her waist. "I thought I might find you here."

"I was watching the storm and hoping it will be over and done with soon."

"No reason to worry when you're in a warm, dry hotel like the Fernhaven."

"So I guess I should stop worrying?"

"Or seek comfort in someone's arms."

She loved his easy ways. It was so different from what she was used to. He was different. Smart. Funny. Rough, yet gentle. It amazed her that the combination could be so sexy. Especially gentleness. Perhaps that was what she loved most about him.

"Sit out the storm with me, Katrina. We can keep

each other company while we listen to the wail of the wind and dance by candlelight."

"What shall we do for music?"

"I always hear music when you're around."

The invitation was the kind of thing dreams were made of—if she'd had the right to dream. She didn't. She reached to her neck and touched the pendant, the reminder that she was here for only one reason and seeking her own happiness wasn't it.

"I can't go with you, Bart."

"Sure you can. I won't do anything you don't want me to do, and that's a promise."

A heated flush shot through her. It was what she wanted him to do that made this whole thing impossible.

"Or I can do anything you want," he said, as if he'd read the torrid hunger that had infiltrated her senses.

"I'm not what you think."

He trailed a finger down her arm. "You've said that before."

"It's still true."

"Then let's not think of truth tonight. Let's not think at all, Katrina. Let's let whatever happens, happen. That can't possibly do you harm."

She wanted to believe him, wanted it so desperately. But she knew he was wrong. Her destiny was already decided, and he wasn't part of it. Still, the desire that coursed through her was so strong. One night. Would it be so wrong to take one night out of all eternity for herself?

She turned and pressed against him. "If I go with you, you have to promise me one thing."

"I'll try."

"When the night's over, you have to let me go and not try to see me again."

He didn't promise. He just touched his lips to hers and she melted so completely, she couldn't fight the attraction any longer. She let him lead her across the dance floor to wherever it was he was taking her. She didn't care. She'd go anywhere with him as long he could feed the storm of passion that rocked her soul.

Chapter Eight

When they exited the elevator on Bart's floor, he swooped Katrina into his arms and carried her down the empty hall to his room. He was excited and nervous, sure he was making a mistake and way too far gone to turn back. He kicked open the door and lay her across the bed.

The west wing would ring with the sounds of talk and laughter soon. All that was left to do was install the carpet in the hall. But for now the wing and the night belonged just to him and Katrina.

"I'll light a candle," he said, trying to think where he'd put the one he'd taken from the dining room.

"No, please. I don't mind the dark."

"You're much too beautiful to be kept in the dark."

"Candles make me nervous."

The alarm in her voice surprised him. He dropped to the bed beside her and let his fingers tangle in the

silky locks of her golden hair. He should say something, whisper the kind of compliments women
loved to hear. Some men did that well. It always
sounded stupid when he'd tried it.

"Why do you want me, Bart?"

"I don't know. I just do. I have ever since that first
night in the ballroom."

"It's the same for me," she whispered. "But I'm
afraid of us, afraid of this."

"I won't hurt you. You surely know that."

"I know. It's just that… Oh, Bart, I don't know
how to do this. I don't know to satisfy you."

"I'm not sure what you're saying, Katrina. You
were married. You must have made love."

"But it wasn't like this. I mean I didn't feel the
way I feel tonight, the way I feel with you…."

That did him in. He wanted to laugh and cry at
the same time. Most of all he wanted to hold her.
"I'm glad, Katrina. I know it's selfish. I don't want
to think of you with another man."

"Oh, Bart. This seems so right, but it isn't real.
It's an illusion. A dream. That's all."

"Then I don't want to wake up."

She wrapped her arms around him. "Let's not
talk anymore, Bart. Just make love with me."

He was so ready, but he couldn't bear the thought
of her having any regrets. "Are you sure you're
ready, Katrina?"

"I've never been more sure of anything."

And neither had he. He kissed her, and then they were a tangle of passion and desire. He couldn't think. He didn't have to. It just all came together.

God, did it come together. He'd thought he'd had great sex before, but it was never like this. He moaned and called her name, over and over, while the hot, ragged need ran wild inside him.

Just when he thought it couldn't get any better, it did. She screamed in passion and he exploded as if someone had lit a firecracker in his bloodstream.

When it was over he held her, glad he'd never made the promise to let her go. But then he felt tears on his chest and he cratered. What if he'd disappointed her? What if she was sorry they'd made love?

"What's wrong, Katrina?"

"Nothing."

"You're crying."

"Tears of joy."

He kissed them away. "If happiness makes tears, then I should be crying, too."

"Not you, Bart Finnegan. I bet you've never cried."

"Not in a long, long time. But I've cried. Men do, you know, but mostly we do it on the inside where it doesn't show."

"If I'd been there when you cried, I would have kissed your tears away like you did mine."

"If you'd been there, there wouldn't have been tears."

She snuggled beside him, then trailed her fingers up and down his chest. "There are things I need to tell you about me, Bart."

"Will I like them?"

"I don't think so."

"Then I don't want to hear them."

"I have to say them."

"Tomorrow. Say them tomorrow."

"Okay, but then you'll have to listen."

"I'll listen, but it won't change how I feel about you. A million daybreaks can come and go, and I'll still want you in my arms."

And drunk or sober, that was undoubtedly the corniest—and truest—words he'd ever uttered.

CARRIE DRIED the last bowl and put it back in the cabinet with the rest of the neatly stacked dishes.

"You do good work, Deputy Fransen. Do you hire out by the day?"

"No. I only work for food. But any time you want to make me another pot of chili, I'll be glad to help with kitchen chores." She untied the borrowed apron and hung it back on the hook next to the pantry. "How did you learn to cook like that?"

"Necessity and watching my grandmother. But my repertoire of menu items is limited. Chili, bacon and eggs, hamburgers and grilled salmon. That's pretty much it, unless you count cereal and canned soup."

"Soup counts. Cereal doesn't unless it's hot cereal. You could earn a couple of brownie points for that."

"Always hated hot cereal. It tastes and looks like something you should feed hogs."

"Raised a lot of hogs, have you?"

"No, but my grandmother made me listen to her read *Charlotte's Web* every time she needed a good cry."

"You must have spent a lot of time with your grandparents when you were growing up. You seem so close to them."

"Just summers and holidays. But I am close to them."

"You're lucky."

"What about you?" he asked.

"I did all right, but I didn't have the storybook kind of grandparents you did."

Or any grandparents for that matter, as least none that stepped forward to take care of her when she was four and her mother had died. No family. No roots. Nothing but a few memories that were from so long ago, she didn't even know if they were real or something she'd made up along the way.

"Where did you grow up?" Rich asked.

"Arizona, near Tucson."

"That's a nice area. How did you end up in Washington State?"

"I worked with an airline. They transferred me here. I liked it and when I decided to go back to school, I worked my way through the University of Washington."

"Go Huskies."

That was the most she'd told anyone with the sheriff's department about her past except Bart. It surprised her that she'd shared it with Rich. Maybe it was the storm and being here in his grandparents' house that made her feel safe enough to talk about it.

"Did your grandmother bake cookies and spoil you rotten?" she asked, switching the focus of their conversation back to him.

He rolled his eyes. "Grandma baked cookies, but there was no spoiling. She made me toe the line. So did my parents except they were always working so I got away with more with them."

"What kind of work did they do?"

"They own a neighborhood restaurant in Seattle. Dad still thinks he has to be there anytime the doors are open, and Mom's almost as bad." Rich opened the doors on one of the higher cabinets and moved a few bottles around. "How about an after-dinner drink? It will help you sleep through the howling wind."

"It does whistle around the corners, doesn't it?"

"Like a screeching owl convention."

"I don't think it will keep me awake, though, not after that hike up the mountain. But the drink offer sounds good. What do you have?"

"Brandy or a peppermint schnapps. The brandy is Granddad's. The schnapps is Grandmother's. That's the only alcohol she drinks, but she loves her nightcap. I've got to remember to buy her a new bottle for Christmas."

"I'll go with your Grandmother's choice."

"You got it." Rich took down two glasses and poured her a couple of fingers of the liqueur and himself a brandy.

She picked up her glass and held it for a toast. "To Tom's speedy recovery," she said, "and a break in the investigation."

"I'll drink to those."

They clinked glasses, and then she took hers back to the living room. Rich followed and added a few more logs to the grate. The old wood sputtered and spit out a few flames in protest, proof they weren't dead yet. Jackson lifted his head to check out the noise that was interrupting his sleep.

Being snowed in with Rich was not as awkward as she'd feared, at least it hadn't been to this point. He was far more patient and thoughtful as a host than as a partner.

Nonetheless, winter storms made strange bedfellows. Without an emergency, she and Rich would never have shared a cozy meal in his grandparents' house or settled in front of a blazing fire for drinks.

And she would never have picked up his grandfather's book of mountain ghost tales. She'd read two stories. They'd frightened her so much, she'd had to put the book down even before Rich had announced the chili was ready.

She picked it up again. "Have you ever read this?" She held the book so Rich could see the title.

"No. I'm a Tom Clancy kind of man. I like details, not hogwash."

"Your grandfather must not think it's hogwash. The books looks well read."

"He's a smart man in lots of ways, but he's superstitious as hell. I hate to admit it, but he's as bad as Maizie is about that undead bull."

"Then he actually believes the stories about the undead roaming the mountains?"

"Afraid so. He also believes in throwing salt over your shoulder, burying beans in the yard to cure warts and knotting your handkerchief to ward off evil spirits."

"You're kidding."

"Cross my heart."

"But you said the two of you spent lots of time in the mountains. Why would he do that if he thought they were haunted?"

"He figured if we didn't bother the undead, they wouldn't bother us. Someone must have told him that, or else he read it in the book you were reading or another one just as stupid."

"I haven't come to that part."

"At any rate, we never encountered a ghost or goblin when we were in the mountains, not even when we camped out."

"If Maizie believes the ghosts are harmless like your grandfather did, then why would she blame them for Tom's mental and physical condition?"

"That's just her. Some people blame the Democrats or Republicans for everything, Maizie blames the mountains. It does offer a lot of immunity from guilt. It's not the pork chops and steaks or the biscuits and gravy that clogged Tom's veins and caused a stroke but some undetermined curse of the mountains."

"She may have some strange ideas, but I like her."

"I like her, too," Rich said. "But it's hard to fathom intelligent people who are reasonable in every other way believing in ghosts."

Which was just the segue way she was looking for to bring up the files they'd examined at Fernhaven. "So what do you make of the complaints of phantasmal happenings at Fernhaven?"

Rich set his empty brandy glass on the mantel and turned his back to the fire. "Talk about your crazies. The Fernhaven must send out flyers to mental hospitals offering free booze and double bonus points."

"So you're ready to dismiss them all?"

"You're not?"

She was—and she wasn't. "What about Marjorie Lipscomb?"

"What about her? She was probably drunk when she called security. She sobered up and withdrew the whole story. What was it she said? She had a nightmare?"

"The report didn't indicate she was drunk."

"It didn't indicate those people who complained about their ice being late or washcloths folded wrong as being pampered jerks, either, but they obviously are."

"Dr. Lipscomb's a renowned psychologist. We had to read her books at the university, and I heard her speak once. Her big thing is dropping inhibitions and fears and taking charge of your life. That hardly makes her the superstitious type."

"I'm not saying she's superstitious," Rich admitted. "I said she was drunk, or maybe popping pills or sniffing a little coke."

The cozy mood they'd shared briefly had totally dissolved. His attitude irritated her, or maybe she was irritated with herself for letting all this haunted lore get to her. Sheriff Powell would yank her off the case before she could say Bippity Boo or knot a handkerchief if he thought she gave the haunted aspect of Fernhaven any credence.

Even Bart would think that was over the line.

Rich kicked off his shoes and perched on the edge of the ottoman, putting them on eye level. "Don't tell me you bought into Marjorie Lipscomb's story."

"I didn't say that."

"Good. We have a killer who's threatened to strike again. We don't have time to go off on a ghost hunt."

"You were the one who suggested going through the complaint files."

"I was looking for something concrete. Someone noticing a man hanging around where he shouldn't be, someone following them or harassing them. I wasn't looking for superstitious booby traps to bog down the investigation."

Rich left the ottoman and stirred the fire, and once again it hit her how well he fit in the house. Sturdy, rugged, no nonsense. Bossy, but she wasn't sure that related to her comparison. He irritated her, but he fit the house and the area.

She tried to imagine him as a young boy listening to his grandmother read *Charlotte's Web*. The image wouldn't gel, but she could easily imagine him out roaming the mountains with his grandfather or as a tough city cop.

"What was it like working homicide in Seattle?"

He propped a booted foot on top of the hearth. "Challenging. Interesting. Sometimes dangerous."

"Why did you leave?"

He stoked the fire again then walked to the window, staring into the night for a few moments before turning back to her. "What did you hear?"

"Nothing, except that you quit."

"I didn't quit. I was let go."

That was news. Powell had acted as if they were privileged to have him. She probably shouldn't ask about the situation, but they'd crossed several lines in their newly established partnership tonight. She might as well state the obvious. "Why did they let you go?"

"I was charged with police brutality."

She stiffened impulsively. He'd finally worked up to tolerable in her book. Now he'd slipped back to ground zero.

Rich turned back to the window. She couldn't see his face, but she saw the muscles bunch in his arms and saw his hands clench into tight fists.

"Aren't you going to ask me about the circumstances or are you just going to judge me from right there on top of your high horse?"

"I wasn't judging." A lie, but what did he expect?

"I used my fists to excess on a punk hoodlum."

Finally he turned to face her, and she could swear she could still see the anger in his eyes.

"He'd just beaten a four-year-old boy to death," Rich continued, his voice strained as if he found it difficult to talk about. "When I asked him about it, he laughed. He laughed, and I lost it."

Her insides knotted. She was sitting here fretting over farfetched stories of supernatural beings. He'd seen the body of a four-year-old who'd been beaten to death. They were on different planes, on different planets. No wonder he looked hard. He'd had to be.

"One of the other punks caught enough of the beating on his cell phone camera that the city had to hold a hearing. Funny thing about punks. They all have guns and cell phones and anything else they can steal."

"Did you fight the charges?"

"Nope. I refused to deny what I did, so I was let go."

She should say something, but only one thing came to mind. "I don't know how you kept from killing him."

"My partner pulled me off."

"What happened to the punk?"

"He was tried as a juvenile. He'll be on the streets again when he's eighteen."

"It seems I'd remember that, but I don't."

"It was a few years back. You were probably away at school. I left law enforcement, roamed the country. Worked on a ranch in Montana for awhile, but then ended up back here when my grandfather had his first heart attack. Sheriff Powell heard I was back and signed me on. Now you know the rest of the story."

It gave her a whole new framework for how she looked at him.

"What do you say we call it a night, Deputy Fransen? You can take my old bedroom. The mattress is newer."

"I say that's a capital idea."

"Bathroom's down the hall. There's only one. The towels on the rods are clean and it takes forever for the water to get hot."

"Thanks."

"You bet. If you need anything during the night, you can squeak. I am a very light sleeper."

She nodded, picked up her glass and started to the kitchen to rinse it and put it in the sink. She was tired. She should fall asleep the second her head hit the pillow.

She made it to the kitchen door before she turned around and went back for the book. Not because she believed in ghosts. It was just good business to know what the locals believed.

One more story, and then she'd turn off the lights and go to sleep, hopefully not to dream of the stories in the book.

THE MATTRESS on his grandparents' bed was old and lumpy, but it was the thoughts pummeling his brain that wouldn't let Rich fall asleep. He'd asked to be put on this case, thought he had something to offer. Now he was beginning to wonder.

The only decent lead they had was Harlan Grant, and he'd slipped right through their hands. Rich had called that all wrong, and his mistake had almost cost Carrie's life. Not that anyone blamed him, but he blamed himself.

He should have arrested Harlan the second he stepped out of that pickup truck. They could have held him twenty-four hours for questioning. He just hadn't figured the guy would head in the woods with two armed cops standing there.

But the real surprise in all of this was Carrie Fransen. He hadn't really liked her before he'd been assigned to this case. She was nice-looking. That was part of the problem. She was too cute. Upbeat. Officer Friendly in person.

But she was a lot more. Bart had figured that out. They'd been more than partners. He just wasn't sure how much more. Not that it mattered or was any of his business.

The important thing was that Carrie was a lot more capable than he'd given her credit for.

He rolled over and punched the pillow a few times, then closed his eyes. The floorboards outside the bedroom creaked. He jerked to a sitting position as a light knock sounded at his door.

"Come in."

"You have to see this, Rich."

It was Carrie, wearing one of his cotton T-shirts and holding that damned ghost book.

"Not more ghosts?"

"It's worse. Much worse." She pushed the book in front of him.

One look and he knew the undead could no longer be ignored.

Chapter Nine

Rich picked up the book for a closer look at the graphic. It was the same symbol, all right, the same squiggly line intersecting with the straight line, appearing just as the cuts had on Elora Nicholas's stomach.

"Do you realize what this means, Rich?"

He probably wasn't thinking what she was. "It could mean any number of things. We have a perp who wants people to think the crimes were committed by a ghost or possibly he thinks he's aligned with the dark side. Or maybe he just saw this symbol somewhere and liked it."

"Did you read what the book says about the symbol?"

He read the caption beneath the drawing out loud. "'The design is a symbol indicating the place where the spirit world and the living intersect. It can be used to represent a physical place or a supernatural event.'"

"A place where the two worlds of the dead and the living mix," she said, paraphrasing the statement. "A place like Fernhaven. This could be a major development, Rich."

He wasn't sure where Carrie was going with this, but he had a feeling it wasn't anywhere he was about to follow.

"It helps narrow down our suspects," he admitted, "and gives us some new clues that might lead to people we wouldn't have considered otherwise. I'm not sure what else it does."

She pulled her feet up on the bed with her and sat cross-legged, facing him and the book. The T-shirt hung off one shoulder, revealing a little too much soft flesh to make this comfortable. Worse he could see the outline of her nipples beneath the worn cotton. He swallowed hard.

Carrie was apparently unaware of the effect she was having on him.

"If there were something to the theory that there are undead in the Fernhaven area, this could represent the killer's intersecting with Elora when he raped her. His world and her world coming together."

"Whoa. Whoa. Whoa!" He moved the book away from her. "You're not suggesting that some dead person who's been wandering around in the mist raped and killed Elora Nicholas. Tell me you're not saying that."

"Not exactly."

"But you think it's possible?"

"I'm just offering a scenario."

"No more liquor for you, Carrie. Or else that bump you took the other night scrambled your brain."

"My brain is fine."

"Then let's sit here and talk like cops." Stupid comment. How could they talk like cops when he was in nothing but a pair of boxers and her nipples were visible through one of his old T-shirts?

"Why don't you grab Grandma's robe and I'll meet you in the kitchen in five?" he said. "We're both wide-awake now. We may as well make a pot of coffee and see if we can make sense of the new information."

"I think the man we're looking for lives in these mountains and believes the way Maizie and your grandfather do. He may have read this same book. He might have eaten in Maizie's café or roamed the same area where we found Tom today?"

"Now I think you could be on to something, Deputy."

Carrie was off his bed and out the door by the time he untangled his legs from the sheet. He wiggled into his jeans and slipped into the old house shoes he'd found in the closet.

He glanced at the book again. A symbol for the

intersection of the spirit world and the living. It was the stuff of horror movies.

Yet it was the symbol their perp had chosen. Bottom line, they might very well be dealing with a killer who lived inside a tortured, demented mind. The thought of ghosts didn't frighten Rich at all. But dealing with a madman was scary as hell.

CARRIE SIPPED her coffee, not that she needed it to stay alert. The adrenaline had started pumping the second she'd found the symbol, and she was still keyed up over what it might mean.

She had to admit that when she'd been alone in her bedroom, ghosts had seemed more than possible. Even now, it didn't seem as farfetched as Rich made it sound.

So many unfortunate souls had burned while trying to escape the death trap when the hotel became an inferno. They'd gone there for a vacation, some on their honeymoon. Most had never gotten a chance to say goodbye to the people they loved.

Now there was a new Fernhaven Hotel, one that was almost identical to the original. Perhaps some of the guests had never totally departed. They might be looking for a way to connect with what they'd lost. And here she went, getting all spooked again. She'd best shape up fast.

She picked up one of the pencils Rich had tossed onto the table, and tapped the eraser end on the tablet he'd scooted in front of her. She kept everything in her head, but Rich was forever making lists.

She stirred a dash of sweetener into her coffee "I guess this rules out Harlan Grant as a suspect. Not likely he'd be exposed to mountain lore in Kansas."

"But he might have been while he was doing time," Rich said. "Prisons have libraries. And he probably had lots of time to read."

"But the symbol can't be all that common. You were raised up here with a superstitious grandfather and you'd never seen it until tonight."

"Actually, I think I might have."

"Say what? You never mentioned that before."

"It was years ago. I couldn't have been more than seven."

"Still, how could you not think of it when you saw Elora's body."

"The one I saw wasn't printed out like the one carved into a body."

"Where was it?"

"Somewhere in the mountains around here. I'm not sure where. Grandpa and I were fishing in one of the mountain streams. I probably got tired of fishing and went off to play. That was pretty much standard routine on our fishing trips. I wandered off, I guess. Anyway I remember coming across this snake-looking thing made out of twigs."

"The symbol?"

"It could have been."

"You've seen the photos of the marks on Elora's body. If you'd seen that design before, why haven't you said something before now?"

"I never connected the two. I was seven. All I remember for sure is the twigs were in a squiggly line."

"Were there any twigs in a straight line?"

"No, but there were some rocks laid out in a straight line."

"A line of rocks that intersected with the twigs?"

"To tell you the truth, I don't remember. Grandpa came looking for me, and when he saw me kicking the twigs, he grabbed me and hauled me back to the truck in double time. He looked so upset, I figured I was in for trouble. But he didn't say anything on the way home and I forgot all about it until now. But if it was the same pattern as the one in that book, then my kicking the twigs would explain his reaction."

"Do you remember where you were when it happened?"

"Nothing other than it was near a mountain stream. Guess I'll have to pay Grandpa a visit as soon as the roads are passable."

"I'd like to go with you."

"Under one condition."

"What's that?"

"You have to promise you won't buy into his superstitions."

"Me? Never. But while we're in Seattle, I think we should try to see Marjorie Lipscomb. Wait," she said, stopping him before he could say no. "I'm not going because I think she saw a ghost that night, I just want to know how the hotel reacted to her story."

"And that would help us because…?"

"Something suspicious is going on at that hotel. Chuck Everly obviously wasn't thrilled at our seeing those complaints the other night. I think the hotel management's hiding something. I just don't know what."

"As long as you don't think they're renting rooms to ghosts."

"Absolutely not. Everyone knows ghosts don't have money."

They went back to work and stayed at it for over an hour, going over things that might help them identify their perp, similar to what a profiler would have done.

Someone not in the mainstream. A loner who was into superstitions and the lore of the undead. Someone who knew his way around the hotel and the grounds. Someone who was a good shot and also skilled with a knife. Someone who'd rape and kill and then write a note begging to be stopped before he did it again.

Finally, the adrenaline wore off, and her eyes grew heavy. Once again, they decided to call it a night. She washed out the coffeepot so it would be ready for morning, then rinsed their cups while Rich put a little more food in Jackson's dog bowl and gave the cur a good ear scratching.

"It's a good thing you're here," she said. "I'd hate to think Jackson would have to sleep outside on a night like this."

"He wouldn't. He's got a warm sleeping spot in the old storage shed and his own door for getting in and out."

"Still he might have been frightened by the howling wind."

"Jackson? He's not afraid of anything, are you, boy?"

Jackson whined his agreement.

"What about you, Rich? Are you afraid of anything?"

He hesitated, as if he had to think about it. "Yeah. I'm afraid. I'm afraid of failing. Afraid that scum like the teenager who killed the little kid in Seattle and some sick son of a bitch who carves symbols on his victims will get away with it. I plan to do all I can to keep that from happening."

She nodded. She believed him, but she still wasn't sure he knew about fear.

"What about you, Carrie? What frightens you?"

Right now it was that way outside chance that they were wrong and that the undead were all around them. She wasn't about to admit that to Rich.

"I'm afraid of spiders and snakes and roller coasters that turn you upside down," she said, none of which was a lie.

But it was the killer she was thinking of as she padded down the hall and back to the warm, cozy bed.

HOSPITALS WERE their loneliest during the wee hours of the morning. There were footsteps outside the door from time to time and occasionally a nurse stopped in to check on Tom or Maizie. She wasn't sure which since Tom was hooked up to a machine that let them monitor his heart from the nurse's desk.

Maizie uncurled from the chair where she'd been dozing off and on since Tom had fallen into a restless sleep. She walked to the window and watched the snow flurries dance in the lights that illuminated the side parking lot and a church beyond that.

The wind had settled down. The snow had, too. It hadn't turned out to be nearly as bad a storm as they'd predicted.

Not a night to be on the roads, though. They were lucky to be here. Lucky that Rich and his partner Carrie Fransen had found Tom when they did. Lucky he was alive.

"Uhhh. Uhhh."

She walked over to the bed and took one of Tom's hands, cradling the bony fingers between her short, chubby ones. "It's okay, Tom. I'm here. You're doing fine."

He didn't open his eyes, but he stopped moaning. She tugged on his top sheet, pulling it out from under his hips and tucking him in like she'd done the kids when they were young.

This wasn't the way she'd pictured them growing old. Tom had always been her rock. He'd taken care of her when she had breast cancer and when she'd nearly died of pneumonia.

Now he was the one who needed tending. She'd warned him time and again about spending so much time out in those woods. She'd quit going camping and fishing with him long ago. Every time she'd gone up there, she'd felt as someone or something was watching her.

The hills were haunted. She'd always had a sixth sense about things like that. Most people didn't. They just went through life unaware that they shared the earth with spirits that weren't confined to time and space.

"Maizie."

"I'm right here, Tom." His eyes were open now, and she moved close enough he could see her face in the glow from the night-light. "I'm not going anywhere until you're ready to go with me."

"I want to go home."

"We will soon."

He turned toward the window. "She's up there."

"Up where?"

"In the mountains."

She pulled a chair next to the bed. "Who's up there, Tom? Who's there?"

"The woman who wants me to help her."

Maizie's chest tightened. She took a deep breath, and it hurt coming in and going out. She didn't know if he was talking about something that had happened today in the mountains, or if he was just talking out of his head.

"Who was the woman, Tom? Who was she?"

"She's trapped up there."

Trapped in the mist. Maizie swallowed past the lump that filled her throat. "What woman?" she whispered, trying to sound calm and to keep the trembling that shook her hands from reaching her voice. "Who was she?"

"I couldn't tell. Her face was gone."

A chilling cold settled in Maizie's heart. All these years, all the time he'd spent in the mountains and he'd never come into direct contact with one of the spirits until this year. Something had changed. The spirits were touching the souls of the living.

It had happened to Tom. It had happened to Selma. It was a bad, bad sign.

CARRIE USED Maizie's phone to call Dr. Lipscomb the next morning at nine. She figured that was the earliest she could be reached at her office number, and she felt more comfortable calling her there than at home.

"Good morning. Dr. Lipscomb's office. How may I help you?"

"I'd like to speak to Dr. Lipscomb."

"Are you one of her patients?"

"Not yet." Though Rich had been ready to commit her for psychiatric care last night.

"She's not available to take calls right now, but I can take your name and phone number and have her call you back."

Carrie gave her the information. The receptionist's attitude changed when she heard the word deputy. "Can you hold on just a minute, Deputy Fransen? I'm not sure if she's with her first patient yet."

Which meant she wasn't. A minute later, Marjorie Lipscomb picked up, and Carrie introduced herself all over again.

"Is this call in reference to one of my patients?"

"No, but I'm very familiar with your work, and I think you could provide some information that might help my partner and I on a murder case we're investigating."

"Have you read my books?"

"Studied them, actually. And I attended one of your lectures at the University of Washington. One of my professors in criminal psychology touted you as one of the most innovative and successful psychologists in the field today. I agree with him."

"That's nice to hear."

"I wonder if my partner and I could come in and talk with you about my case."

"I should have an opening one day next week."

"I was thinking more like tomorrow. This is really urgent."

"I'm pretty sure my appointment schedule is full."

"If you could fit us in any time at all, we'd really—"

"No, wait. I might be able to squeeze you in for a few minutes at 10:30 tomorrow. Is that convenient?"

"Perfect. We'll see you then."

Carrie hung up the phone and breathed a sigh of relief. She'd gotten the appointment without mentioning the Fernhaven Hotel. That had been Rich's idea, one of his better ones, though he still thought talking to the doctor was a waste of time. But this way they'd be able to read her reaction when they brought up the incident she'd reported at the hotel.

The smell of bacon wafted in from Maizie's kitchen. The café was closed due to Tom's hospitalization and the storm, but Rich had raided Maizie's refrigerator once again and he'd promised Carrie the best bacon-and-cheese omelet she'd ever eaten. She didn't tell him she'd never had a bacon-and-cheese omelet. She was a bagel and coffee gal. If she kept eating like this, she'd have to order a bigger uniform.

She stared out the window at the snow that covered the world like frosting. In the bright light of day, looking at the snow, smelling bacon—she could almost forget the way her stomach had churned and her blood had run cold when she'd discovered the symbol last night.

KATRINA WALKED through the snow, loving the way it felt beneath her feet and the way the sun glistened on the pure white surface. She took one of the secluded paths that led to the private cabins. She didn't usually venture that far but she had to get away from the hotel today, away from Bart.

Making love with him had been beautiful and perfect. Even in her dreams, she'd never imagined that anything could have made her feel the way she did when they'd become one. She'd trade a lifetime for one more night like that, if she'd had a lifetime to trade.

Already she ached for him. And she'd lied when she'd said the tears were tears of joy; they were pieces of her heart melting and breaking away.

How could fate be so cruel? How could it give her Bart for one night when all of this was about to be ripped away from her? Time was running out. It was down to hours now, maybe days if she was lucky. But if she became sidetracked from what she had to do, it might all be over in an instant.

Over. Once again.

She reached into her pocket and wrapped her hand around the pendant. It was hot to the touch now, as if the fire were already seeping into it. She hated to think about that night, but it was taking over now, the way it did so frequently. Time disintegrated as if it had never passed.

THE MUSIC drifted up from the ballroom. She stood in front of the mirror, checking her hair and her dress. And then she took the pendant from the jewelry box and fastened it around her neck. It was so beautiful, the family heirloom, an amulet passed on to every daughter when she married. It empowered them, guaranteed they always had something in life to fall back on.

The door to their hotel room opened and her husband stepped in. He'd been drinking. She could smell the whiskey on his breath even before he put his lips to the back of her neck.

She'd only seen him drunk once. He'd gone crazy, accused her of all sorts of things. And then he'd sobered up and brought her flowers to make it up to her.

He circled her waist, then let his hands ride up and cup her breasts. He pinched, and she pulled away.

"Don't. Please."

"Don't what? Don't touch you? I'm your husband now, Katrina. You belong to me. And I'll touch you any time I please."

"Please don't act this way. You frighten me when you drink."

"Do I, now?"

"Yes." She pulled away, but he stuck his hands beneath her skirt and started pinching her thighs, so hard it brought tears to her eyes.

"It's our honeymoon, Jonathan. Please don't spoil it."

"You've already done that. Do you think I didn't see you looking at that man you were talking to in the garden? You did everything but invite him up here to screw you."

"Don't talk like that."

"You're a slut."

"That's not true. I was only making conversation. It's the whiskey. You only talk like this when you've been drinking."

"Get used to it. I plan to drink a lot, my little bride. And I will talk any way I want."

"Then I'm leaving."

"Like hell you are." He grabbed her and threw her onto the bed. Her head slammed against the bedpost and her vision went fuzzy.

She kicked him and ran for the door. If this was

marriage, she wanted no part of it. She'd rather be an old maid all her life than be treated like this.

He grabbed her arm as she reached the door and twisted it behind her back.

"Let go of me, Jonathan, or I'll leave you. I swear I'll leave and I won't come back."

"You prima donna whore. You think you're something with that Fort Knox rock hanging around your neck. Well, let me tell you something. Nobody walks out on me. And you can kiss this goodbye."

The chain of the necklace cut into her neck as he ripped it from her. She went at him with both fists flying. But he was too quick. The crystal lamp base came down on her head.

She tried to get up, but the room was spinning and her legs wouldn't move.

"I'll see you in hell, Katrina, but you'll be there long before me."

She watched in horror as he held the burning candle to the drapes, the flame licking at the fabric until it ignited. She was going to die on her honeymoon. Murdered by the man who'd promised to cherish her for the rest of her life.

THE NECKLACE in Katrina's pocket was so hot she could barely stand to touch it now. She left the path and started to run through the woods. She didn't know where she was going. She didn't care.

"KATRINA. Katrina, stop."

She didn't and Bart took off after her, determined not to lose her in the lush growth of young evergreens. He'd been only a few steps behind her, about to surprise her with a kiss when she'd bolted and run.

"Katrina. Wait!"

She was faster than he was. It was as if she floated over the snow, so light she didn't sink into it with every step the way he did.

He stopped and leaned against a tree. He didn't have the strength to run like this. He shouldn't be running at all in his condition.

He could barely stand. But then he heard her crying, and he found the strength to push ahead. She was hugging a tree, crying into her fists. The pain he'd felt from running was nothing compared to what he felt at seeing her like this.

He took her in his arms and held her close. "What's wrong, Katrina?"

"Everything."

"I'm here now. We'll make it right."

"Oh, Bart. I wish that were true, but you can't make it right. No one can."

"Try me."

She pulled away from him. "Look at me, Bart. Take a very good look. I'm not what you think I am."

"I think you're…"

"No. No more pretense." She backed away from

him, but her gaze held firm. "I'm the Katrina O'Malley in the picture, and I died in the Fernhaven Hotel seventy years ago."

Chapter Ten

Bart stared at Katrina, shocked and hurt by her words. "Why are you saying these things?"

"I have to say them. They're true."

"Look, Katrina, I don't know what's going on with you, but if you're in some kind of trouble I can help you. I'm a cop. But I can't do anything unless you level with me."

"I know how this sounds. Believe me, I know you must think I'm a mental case, but I'm telling you the truth."

"No." He couldn't believe this. He wouldn't. She was afraid and she'd concocted this bizarre story so he'd walk away and forget her.

"Listen to me, Katrina. Whatever you've done, we'll find a way through it. Just let me help you."

"Oh, Bart, I wish that you could, but nothing can help."

She bit her bottom lip, but still tears filled her

eyes. Not tears of joy this time. He was pretty damn sure of that. He reached out to take her in his arms. She pulled away.

"I should have told you the truth from the beginning," she said. "This is all my fault. I should never have let it go this far."

"Why didn't you?"

"I wanted to be with you. I knew it couldn't last. I just wanted to feel alive, to feel you."

"You are alive. I see you. I touched you. I made love with you. Now give up this ridiculous charade, and let me help you."

"I can't."

"Do you trust me?"

"It's not a matter of trust. It's a matter of truth."

"Did you take something? Have you been on drugs?"

"No, Bart. You want an easy answer, but there's not one. I'm dead. And I'll be leaving this place soon."

"I won't let you go."

She started to sob, and this time when he reached for her, she melted in his arms.

He didn't know what was going on, but he couldn't let her go. He couldn't lose her. What he knew about love, you could put on the back of a postage stamp in large block letters. But he'd connected with Katrina in a way he'd never connected with anyone before, and he refused to give her up before they had a chance.

"Go back to my room with me. We'll talk," he pleaded.

"That will only make it harder."

"You're not dead, Katrina. And you weren't in this hotel seventy years ago. You're young and vibrant with no signs of age."

"Time doesn't exist in my world. It folds and wrinkles and doubles back on itself, but it has no permanence."

"If there's no time, then stay with me."

"I can't. I don't control that."

"Why do you think you're dead?"

"I don't think it. I know it, but I didn't realize it at first. It was only when no one saw me, when rescuers walked up to me, felt my wrist, and then walked on by that I began to think I might have died in the fire."

"But I see you, Katrina."

"That happens sometimes. When it does I leave, the way I should have done with you. I never meant to hurt you, Bart. I never meant to let you get so close. You have to forget me. It's the only way."

"Forget you? Do you know what you're asking? You came into my life and took over my body and soul, and now you think you can just walk away, and I'll forget you. It may be that way in that crazy world you've concocted in your mind, but it's not that way in mine."

"I have to go."

Her words were a strained whisper. She was hurting, but so was he. He couldn't get through to her, couldn't find a common ground. It was as if they spoke two different languages. The words sounded the same, but they had different meanings.

She pulled away from him, then put her hand to his cheek. "I love you, Bart, but the love came years too late."

He closed his eyes, fighting his own bitter tears. When he opened them, Katrina was gone. He didn't chase after her this time. He had to think, had to sort this out in his mind.

He started back to the hotel, but he couldn't go back to his room. He couldn't bear to have the memory of making love to her torment him.

He went back to the winding path and followed it to the most remote cabin, the one that sat near the ravine where Elora Nicholas's body had been found. He could disappear into the woods there and be totally alone.

Katrina was tearing him apart, but he couldn't give into the grief. He still had a killer to find.

CARRIE AND RICH were on the highway just before noon. She'd been impatient, but Rich had assured her that this was far earlier than the snowplows would have cleared the roads in this area before the new hotel had been up and running. The owners of the hotel obviously had clout.

They'd made stops at two of the names on his list of locals. The first was a widow who'd taught history at the local high school for thirty years before retiring a year ago. She knew lots of mountain lore, but none of it concerned the spirit world. She'd never heard anything about an intersection of the two worlds and if she had, she would have dismissed it as rubbish.

Her late husband had spent hundreds of hours in the very spot where the first hotel had burned down searching for valuables lost in the fire. He wasn't the only one. Years ago, scouring the area with metal detectors had been a major weekend activity.

As far as she knew, none of the seekers had ever had ghostly experiences, except maybe some of the hippies who were tripping out.

She was convinced that Elora Nicholas had been murdered by someone new to the community. Basically, it was a result of the hotel and the influx of people it had brought to their little corner of the world.

All of which was interesting, but no help.

The second stop had been at the home of Ben Getts, a retired plumber from Seattle. He and his wife had finally packed it in and moved to their mountain cottage. He'd actually done some work on the Fernhaven when it was being built. Apparently Owen Billings had worked with the roofing crew, and he'd gotten the plumber a job laying pipes for the numerous fountains in the garden and along the paths to the cabins.

The man knew of the problems Owen's wife was having. He was sympathetic, but he wrote it off as a problem with depression and overdosing on pills.

"A wasted afternoon," Rich said, when they finally hit the highway again. "We've got a time bomb inside a killer's head, and we're hitting nothing but brick walls."

Carrie grabbed a tissue from her pocket just in time to catch a sneeze.

"Bless you."

"Thanks."

"Sounds as if you're coming down with a cold."

"I'm pretending I'm not," she said, "but I wish we could have talked to your grandfather and to Dr. Lipscomb today instead of having to wait until tomorrow."

"It will be late afternoon before all the roads are cleared and safe for driving."

"Do you have any more names on your list?"

"A couple, but they can wait." Rich adjusted his sun visor to better block the late afternoon sun. "I'd like to go back to the hotel and have a look around those outer cabins again before dark. I have a strong hunch that if the killer strikes, it will be there instead of the main hotel."

"I have that same hunch. They're a much easier target than the main hotel, especially since all the new security's been added."

"You can stay inside if you like. No use to be out in the weather if you're already getting sick."

"I'll take that offer. I'd like to find Jeff Matthews and hopefully take a look at some of his snapshots. I don't expect it to help with the investigation, but it can't hurt."

"Careful with Jeff Matthews."

"You're surely not thinking of him as a possible suspect?"

"I haven't ruled out anyone."

"I can handle him."

"He'd like to handle you."

"What does that mean?"

"Guy's got the hots for you."

"C'mon. No way."

"Believe me. Guys can tell. He wants your body."

"I'll sneeze all over him a few times. That should eliminate the lust factor."

But even if it didn't. Carrie was not afraid of Jeff Matthews. Her only fear was that he and his pictures would be yet another dead end.

JEFF'S ROOM was luxurious, with white down comforters on the two single beds and fluffy pillows in forest-green cases to match the sheets. There was a huge dresser, a love seat and chair in cherry wood and a woodsy print and a large round table with a beautiful glass-and-metal lamp.

The view was the only thing that indicated the room might be at the lower end of the pricing scale. His window looked out over the employee parking lot, though it did offer a glimpse of the edge of the garden.

"You've been busy," she said, turning so that she could take in the array of snapshots that plastered every piece of furniture in the room and took up a great deal of the floor space.

"I'm trying to decide which ones to use."

"Do you always take so many shots?"

"No. I usually take about a third this many."

"Did you find Fernhaven that fascinating?"

"Absolutely. I hate to leave."

"Then you must have no complaints about the service or your accommodations?" She was fishing, though she didn't know if she wanted more ghost stories or assurance that he hadn't encountered any disembodied or apparitional spirits.

"I have one. For this price, I should have had some young starlet tuck me into bed every night and then crawl in with me to keep me warm."

Rich had been wrong. Jeff didn't have the hots for her. He just had the hots, period. Any woman would do. She walked to the desk and picked up a snapshot of the exquisitely carved domed ceiling that topped the Glacier Ballroom.

"It's a work of art," Jeff said.

"It's beautiful, and your picture captures it well."

"That's one of many. I spent a lot of time in the ballroom. Full or empty, it had a mystical ambiance about it. Unfortunately, ambiance is the most difficult element to capture on film."

"That's why I never take pictures," she admitted. "The image in my mind is always far more potent that the one I get from my camera." She put down that picture and picked up one that had been taken in the garden. "That looks like sparkling raindrops," she said, running her finger over a spot on the edge of the photograph.

"It's spray from the fountain. I had to take that picture a dozen times at a dozen different times of the day to get it to come out right."

"And you go to all that trouble for your travel articles?"

"No, the articles are to keep me from being a starving artist. These are pure art."

"You should find a gallery in Seattle to showcase your photographs."

"I'm working on it."

She moved from the desk to the round table beneath the window. She went through a new stack of photos, but these were all taken around the waterfall. Some were just magnificent scenery. Another showed a mother tugging her small son back from the edge. You could see the alarm in her eyes and the wonder in the child's face.

The pictures were intriguing, but they weren't getting her anywhere. She was ready to thank him for his time when she came across a shot that turned her stomach. It was a couple going at it in one of the hot springs near the cabins. It was dark, but you could still see a lot more of their naked bodies than Carrie wanted to see.

"Sorry. I didn't realize that was in there."

Jeff tried to take it from her, but she held on. "I know that woman. She's..." Her mind drew a blank, but she was certain she knew the woman from somewhere. Then it hit her. "She's on a sitcom."

"She could be."

"No, not could be. She is. And you're not here for your art or your articles. You're a nosy, voyeuristic paparazzi."

"You make paparazzi sound like a dirty word."

"That's because it is."

"Hey, I just snap the pictures. It's the millions of scandal-hungry fans that shell out cash for the tabloids every week that keep the business afloat."

"But you are the one who violates the person's right to privacy."

"It's called survival. A picture like that can feed me for a month. Besides, the print version won't be that revealing. They have to keep them clean enough to make the grocery shelves."

But her image of Jeff as a talented, yet-to-be discovered artist had been shattered, and the new image galled her. "I'm out of here, Mr. Matthews. Thanks for your time, and I'd advise you to check out of the hotel immediately. If not, I'll be forced to tell them how you're violating the privacy of their other guests."

"I can't believe you're that bent out of shape over one picture. And, hard as it may be for you to believe, the actress will love the exposure, pun intended. If she was modest, she wouldn't be going at it in a public place."

He had a point, but that didn't make his behavior any more acceptable.

"Wait. I know you don't like my tactics, but I have a few pictures I think you should see." He picked up a brown envelope from the desk and handed it to her.

She loosed the clasp and slid the pictures onto the table. The first one was the snapshot he'd taken of her sitting on the bench in the garden, but there were at least a dozen more, all of her.

In the second one, she was waiting for a hotel elevator. Most of the picture was in perfect focus, but there was one fuzzy area, as if someone had spilled something on the print.

She skimmed the rest of the pictures, all taken in

various parts of the hotel or the grounds. And in every picture, there was a blot of some kind, indistinct, but vaguely in the shape of a person.

That was odd, since the other pictures he had on display were perfect. But even creepier was the fact that he had taken so many shots of her.

"Have you been stalking me?"

"You might say that."

"Why?"

"You make an interesting picture, don't you think?"

"Why did you blur the shots?"

He leaned against the window frame. He was looking right at her, but he'd lost his boyish smile. "I didn't blur the shots. I took a clear image. That's the way they came out."

"There must have been something on your camera lens."

"I'm a professional photographer. My lenses are spotless."

"Then how do you explain this?" she asked, trailing her finger over one of the flaws.

"I can't. I was hoping you could."

He was serious, or he was a darn good actor.

"I don't have a clue," she admitted.

"It's as if you have some kind of aura that's so strong, it's visible to the camera. Sometimes it seems dark. Other times it exudes a faint glow. But then you can see that for yourself."

She could see it, but there had to be a reasonable explanation. "Maybe it's the light here in the mountains. You must have had the same problem when you photographed other people?"

"It happened a time or two, but never as strong or as consistent as with you."

"It must be your camera." Or else he was playing tricks with her mind.

"I'm as confused by this as you are," Jeff said. "But there's more." He opened one of the drawers below the TV cabinet and took out another brown envelope, this one much larger than the one that had held her photographs.

"Take a look at this," he said, handing her a photo that had been taken near the garden gazebo.

She wasn't in the picture. Neither was anyone else, yet a human-shaped blur appeared to be sitting on the iron bench. And the eerie glow was more pronounced than ever, as if someone were holding a candle underneath the photograph.

"Then it's not my aura."

"Not in this picture."

"So how do you explain it this time?"

"I can't."

She studied Jeff. His expression, stance and demeanor suggested he was telling the truth. She had to get out of here, had to breathe fresh air and think clearly. "I need the pictures of me, Jeff."

"Sure. Take them. I have the negatives."

She grabbed them and all but ran from the room. Even as she did, she had the strange feeling that someone was watching her.

This was crazy. Or maybe she was going crazy, losing her touch with reality the way Tom and Selma had. *I'm not your patient yet, Dr. Lipscomb, but if this keeps up I will be soon.*

She fell against the wall by the elevator. *Oh, Bart, why in the devil aren't you here now?*

He wasn't, so she had to do this herself, and she couldn't do it by running away. That's why she'd become a cop in the first place, so she wouldn't run from life and responsibility, so she'd take charge of her life and use her new strength for good.

Empowerment came from within. She'd learned that from one of Dr. Lipscomb's books.

She'd start taking more control tonight. Rich probably wouldn't approve, but that was his problem. She would do what she had to, and just maybe it would help her get closer to finding the killer before he struck again.

HARLAN SHRANK back into the woods when he saw the pretty young deputy on the secluded path that meandered through the thick forest of evergreens. He couldn't see much of her all bundled up in that green parka the way she was, but he could imagine how she looked beneath that and the uniform.

All business on the outside, but he bet she

wasn't underneath the deputy camouflage. Satin panties. Yeah. That's what she'd wear. Red satin, with a border of red lace. And women like her always wore thong panties.

She'd look great in them. Tempting to a hungry man. And he was hungry now. And there was no one around but the two of them.

Even if she screamed, no one would hear her. She might not scream. She might like it as much as he did. And he would like it. He needed it. A man could stay in hiding only so long without a little something to keep him going.

And it was her fault. If she hadn't come after him that night and taken him by surprise, he could have thought things through better. They didn't have anything on him. But he'd panicked and now he was holed up in the woods, living in that pickup truck like a freakin' mountain man.

She was only a few yards from him now, so close he could smell her perfume. Things started happening in his head. Just like before. Happening fast. Red satin panties. He could see them. Young, hot flesh.

He reached into his pocket and pulled out the knife. She was only a step away.

Chapter Eleven

Carrie heard movement and spun around. Impulsively, her hand flew to the butt of the gun. "Who's there?"

There was no response.

Probably a squirrel, maybe even a bird. Her nerves were shot, and that was not the preferred operating mode for a cop on a murder case. She turned and looked back down the path she'd just walked.

One of the utility carts the workers used for shuffling supplies and guests about the resort was bumping its way toward her. Rich. She took a deep breath, trying to pull herself together before she faced him.

He pulled to a stop right next to her. "I thought you were staying inside and warm."

"I got bored," she lied. "And I have news."

"Good. Me, too," he said. "Hop in."

"You go first," she said, when she'd settled onto the padded seat.

He pressed the pedal and they started back toward the hotel. "I got a call from Maizie. Tom's doing great. If it continues, they'll release him in the morning."

"That's terrific."

"Now let's hear your news."

"I'm not going home tonight."

He shot her a dubious look. "Tell me this doesn't mean you're hooking up with the grinning camera boy."

"Men don't make passes at girls who wear weapons."

"Not unless they get half a chance."

"I'm not staying with Jeff, but I do have accommodations here at the Fernhaven."

"Yeah, right."

"I'm serious."

"You don't have to work twenty-four hour shifts, you know. There is a night crew, not to mention that the current Fernhaven security rivals the National Guard for manpower."

"And now they'll have their own deputy on the premises."

They came to a Y and he took the path that cut back to the hotel. "Then I hope you're willing to give up a week's salary for every night you stay because there's no way Powell is going to okay that kind of expenditure. He's got budget woes as it is."

"That's the really swell part of all of this," she

said, trying to sound positive. "The hotel is so appreciative of my efforts and so thankful for my offer that they're comping a few nights."

"Nice work, Fransen." He high-fived her. "How about negotiating my next contract?"

"Wouldn't help. Powell's much tougher than the hotel."

"So, when do you move in?"

"Oh…" She made a show of checking her watch. "Somewhere about now."

"Not even going home for a change of clothes?"

"I don't have to. The hotel laundry provides overnight service, and the hotel has gift packs for those of us who forgot to pack the basics, such as toothbrush and razor."

"Sounds like a much better deal than you got last night."

"No homemade chili."

"Well, there's that." He drove around to the back and parked near the employee entrance. "Then I guess you're all set."

"I am."

"Let's go have a look at the room. I've been dying to bounce on one of those beds."

"It's not actually a room."

"Ah, a broom closet," he said. "Never mind about negotiating my contract."

"Not a broom closet, either, though it looked as if that might be among my choices. The hotel is totally booked, and since the roads into Seattle and the airport weren't fully plowed, no one left. The only opening is in one of the cabins. Apparently the guests there had a helicopter fly in and pick them up after the blizzard."

"Which cabin?"

"Number twelve."

"Number twelve as in the very remote and isolated cabin nearest the murder site."

"Yeah. Lucky me."

"And me," he said, jumping out of the cart and heading for the door.

She followed him. "How do you figure?"

"A good cop never runs out on his partner. And I am a hell of a cop."

DINNER IN the hotel restaurant had been great, but now that they were back in the cabin, things were awkward. Two nights together was probably pushing things, especially with both of them on the edge with the investigation.

One step forward; two steps back. And now the backward steps were taking them into uncertain territory. Rich couldn't rule out that the abduction and murder had been some kind of ritualistic killing, and that more than one person might be involved. The note saying the killer wanted to be stopped might just be an effort to throw them off.

He didn't have a good handle on the crime, and

he wasn't even sure he had a good handle on Carrie. She was more complex than he'd imagined. Smarter, too. She had a good mind for seeing clues. But she was also vulnerable. She missed Bart, and she was spooked by the talk of the undead and especially by the marking the killer had used as his signature.

He could understand it. He'd grown up with the superstitions. When you were around people who believed in the supernatural, they could make the impossible seem so real. When he was a kid, they'd only talked about it in quiet voices when they thought he wasn't around.

But he'd picked up the fear and heard enough that it had scared him to death, especially when those college women had been slaughtered. Fortunately, his parents had been level-headed nonbelievers, and he'd finally realized the haunted business was a crock.

But it was all new to Carrie, and she was being hit with it full force. The ridiculous complaints about the hotel definitely hadn't helped. Most of them had been about totally insignificant things, the spoiled rich suffering the indignities of a bed that wasn't made to suit them or a distaste for the brand of chocolates left on their beds at turndown.

Still, a few had come right out of a horror novel, especially Marjorie Lipscomb's. But it was classic for the situation. If you came to the hotel focusing on the fact that it was a near replica of a hotel that had burned down in the same spot, you'd have nightmares. He took most shrinks for being a little on the weird side anyway. Why else would they want to dig around in other people's sick minds?

Then again, some people might question why people went into law enforcement when it meant getting shot at by sickos and punks. Some days he questioned it himself. This wasn't one of them. This was one of those cases that got under his skin like a fungus, driving him crazy. A man who'd carve a marking like that into a woman might do anything—anything at all.

He pulled his black notebook from his pocket and flipped to the list he'd started this afternoon. Possible motivation. This was the list that worried him most. The motivating factors for raping, killing and carving a woman with a mark of the fabled undead never came up as sane.

Carrie shuffled through the newspaper for the second time, not reading a word. She was as restless as he was, too tangled up in the case to think of anything else. She was a good cop. She'd make a great one someday.

He hadn't seen it before. He'd thought Bart was coddling her along, making all the decisions. But Bart had no doubt seen her potential. And if he saw more and had gotten entangled with an attraction for her, who could blame him? Intelligence, curiosity, drive and looks. It was a hard combination to beat even before you threw in her sense of humor and femininity.

Carrie tossed the newspaper she'd been reading to the table.

"I think I'll go outside and get some fresh air."

"Be easier if we just open a window," he said.

"No use to let the cabin get cold." She took her parka from the coat rack by the door and slipped it on.

"Do you want company?"

"I'll be fine alone. I won't be long."

He watched her go, tempted to join her but not sure he should. If it had been a guy partner, he wouldn't even have thought about walking outside with him, so it probably shouldn't be different with a woman.

Rich started a new list. Where Harlan could have disappeared to since he hadn't been spotted.

Number one was the obvious. He could still be in the immediate area. There were acres and acres of woods where a man could hide, but not without food. Sooner or later, he'd have to come out of the mountains for food.

He started another new list. Most likely places for Harlan to show up. Number one was to break in a house when he knew no one was around. Rich continued the list, but by the time he reached five, he was thinking a lot more about Carrie than he was Harlan Grant.

He yanked his parka off the hook. He was going out to check on her. If she didn't want his company, she'd tell him.

He found her standing at the edge of the clearing and staring into the woods in the direction where Elora Nicholas had been murdered.

She sniffed, and he wondered if it was the cold or if she'd been crying.

"You okay?"

She nodded, but didn't turn around. "I'm just thinking."

"About Elora?"

"No, I was thinking about how quiet it is out here. Bart said that when they had a quiet night back in L.A., they'd figure the criminals were resting up for a crime spree, but that quiet in northern Washington was a good thing."

"You and Bart made quite a team."

"We did."

"You must miss him."

"A lot. I worked my first investigation with him. I thought I knew it all. He let me know quick that I didn't, but he did it without making me feel like a fool. After that, he became my full-time mentor. Worked out great since neither of us had anyone else to go home to at night."

"Being alone can be tough at times."

She pulled a tissue from her pocket and dabbed at her nose, then finally she turned and faced him. "Were you ever married?"

"Twice."

"What happened?"

"My first wife left me after a year, said she wasn't ready to settle down. Actually she was, just not with me. She married her dentist."

"Ouch. What happened the second time?"

"The second one left because she said I was not over wife number one."

"Were you?"

"Who knows? Anyway I figure with two strikes on me, I better be damned sure of the results before I swing again."

"So you're waiting for Mrs. Right?"

"Naw. I'm looking for a good-looking slut who likes sex, beer and the Seahawks."

"You know what, Deputy McFarland? I don't think you're nearly as tough and as hard as people think you are."

"Well, don't spread that word at headquarters. You'll ruin my bad reputation. Now, I think we should go in. I don't want you getting sicker and trying to shirk your responsibilities. We still have a killer to catch and a trip into Seattle first thing tomorrow morning."

As it turned out, Carrie got to make the call on Dr. Marjorie Lipscomb all by herself. Rich had driven into the city with her, but he was meeting with one of his old buddies from the Seattle Police Department to discuss an investigation the man had headed up two years ago involving some kids who'd formed a gang that practiced devil worship.

The only time the detective could meet with him today was the exact same time as their appointment with Dr. Lipscomb. All for the best, Carrie figured. The doctor might open up more in a one-on-one interview with someone who wasn't as diametrically opposed to belief in the supernatural as Rich was.

Carrie arrived early, but she was kept waiting until nearly eleven. The doctor's private office was impressive and a little daunting. There were no couches, just her desk, a couple of tan easy chairs and a large brass lamp with a cream-colored shade.

Awards, certificates and diplomas plastered the back wall. The side walls held floor-to-ceiling shelves crammed full of books.

Dr. Lipscomb was even more impressive than her office and looked younger than she had several years ago when Carrie had attended her lecture. She was middle-aged, probably fifty or near it, blond, chic and wearing a white leather skirt and pale pink blouse that capitalized on her great figure.

They shook hands, exchanged introductions and Carrie told her once again how much she'd learned from her books.

"That's always nice to hear." She took a seat behind her desk and motioned Carrie to one of the tan chairs. "Now exactly what is this case that you think I may be able to assist you with?"

Now came the fun part, but Carrie had rehearsed this well on the drive in. "I'm investigating the case involving the woman who was abducted from the Fernhaven Hotel."

"Yes, I heard about that. Very sad. So exactly how do you think I can help?"

Carrie leaned forward in her chair and waited until the doctor's gaze locked with hers. "I know that you spent a long weekend at the Fernhaven about a month ago."

The doctor's expression didn't change, but there was a noticeable surge in tension in the room. Carrie would have to go easy if she wanted the doctor to be honest about what she'd really seen and heard that night at the hotel.

"I stayed there, but I didn't realize my vacations warranted notice by the sheriff's department."

"We've examined some of the hotel records as part of the investigation. It's routine in this kind of case, and we honor the hotel's policy of keeping guest information confidential."

"When you requested this appointment, you indicated it was to ask my professional opinion not to question me about my stay at the hotel."

"Yes, I know. And I do want your professional opinion."

"I'd like to help you, Deputy Fransen, but I'm very busy. So what is your specific question?"

"I'd like to know more about the complaint that someone broke into your room during the night."

"If you read my file, as you obviously did, you know that I recanted. I was taking medication for a sprained muscle and that combined with the wine I had for dinner brought on a very vivid and lifelike nightmare. There's not a lot else I can do with that for you, either professionally or as a layman."

Carrie had definitely struck a nerve. Dr. Lipscomb was clearly agitated, and Carrie doubted that happened too often in a professional setting.

Now Carrie felt like the psychologist searching for the right manner to diffuse the situation and get the doctor to open up. "I've had that same problem before. One drink with a pill, and my system goes whacko. But the weird thing is, other people have made very similar reports to yours."

"The hotel didn't admit that to me. They seemed shocked at my complaint."

They would. "I realize it could have been a nightmare," Carrie continued. "It's just unusual that other people have claimed similar experiences. That's why it would help if you could tell me more about your original complaint."

The doctor's perfect composure started to fade.

She exhaled and spread her hands flat on her desk. "What is it you want to know?"

"You said that a woman came running into your room. Do you remember what she looked like?"

Dr. Lipscomb dropped the pen and clasped her hands. Her lips were drawn tight now, and the creases around her eyes had deepened.

"She was dressed in a nightgown, the old-fashioned kind that had lace at the neck and sleeves and hung loose all the way to her ankles. Her hair was gray, but long, almost to her waist."

"What did she do when she came in?"

"She started screaming at me, telling me that the hotel was on fire, and that if I didn't get out quickly, I'd burn to death. And then she touched..."

"What did she touch?"

"She touched my shoulder, and her hand was red-hot." Dr. Lipscomb rubbed her shoulder as if she could still feel the heat.

"Did she say or do anything else?"

"No. That's when I woke up. The nightmare seemed so real, I ran into the hall. When I didn't see any flames, I called security. They assured me there was no fire, but they'd register my complaint."

"And the next morning you recanted it all."

"Yes."

"You never thought the woman might be a ghost?"

"Most definitely not. If I said anything like that,

it was the mixture of alcohol and medication talking. Now you'll have to forgive me. I really must get back to my clients."

She'd closed up again. Carrie doubted she'd get anything else out of her, but she'd heard enough that her stomach was tying itself into painful knots.

Dr. Lipscomb was freaked out big time over what she'd seen or thought she'd seen in the hotel that night. For the public record, she's said it was a nightmare, but anyone watching her tell that story would know differently. She believed that a woman had come into her room.

Rich McFarland didn't believe supernatural powers he couldn't prove or disprove. If Bart were around, he'd tell her the same thing. There were no ghosts or spirits or places where the undead intersected with the living.

But what if they were all wrong and Rich's grandfather and Maizie Henderson were right?

Now Carrie really couldn't wait for their visit with Rich's grandparents. His grandfather might be the best one around to give insight as to the symbol and the bizarre happenings at Fernhaven.

RICH'S GRANDPARENTS were as warm and welcoming as their house had been. Rich had stopped for to-go orders of fish and chips, his grandparents' favorite, and the four of them had laughed and talked their way through lunch. They covered Tom, Maizie,

Jackson and the fact that Carrie and Rich had spent the night in their mountain home during the storm. Mrs. McFarland seemed especially pleased about that.

Carrie couldn't help but let the envy creep in. She would have thought she was in heaven to have grandparents like this when she was growing up. She'd missed that chance.

By the time she'd moved out of her foster parents' home and researched her ancestry, both of her grandparents were dead. She wasn't sure they'd even known she existed.

Her mother had been the only child of a mother who'd been an only child. The best information she could gather indicated that her own mother had left home to find herself and never returned. Instead she'd gotten pregnant by a man whose name hadn't been included on Carrie's birth certificate.

When she'd died in a head-on car collision, Carrie had been taken as a ward of the court. As best she could tell, her paperwork had fallen through the cracks and her grandparents had never been tracked down and notified they had a granddaughter.

Now that she'd met Rich's grandparents, she planned to picture hers just this way. Well, except maybe for the superstitions.

When the last fry was eaten, his grandmother got up to clear the table.

"Let me do that," Carrie said, jumping up to help.

"No. You just stay right there and relax. This is the only exercise I get all day. I have some chocolate cake for dessert. I baked it just yesterday."

"Now that's what I'm talking about," Rich said. "Bring it on."

Mrs. McFarland's smile claimed her face. "Who wants coffee with their dessert?"

Carrie picked up her plate. Mrs. McFarland took it away from her. "Kitchen's only big enough for one."

"Give it up," Rich said. "Grandma always wins any argument."

His grandfather laughed. "You got that right."

They all opted for coffee, and Rich waited until his grandmother was in the kitchen before he brought up the subject of the symbol they'd found in the book. He didn't mention that it had been carved on the victim, nor had that bit of information ever been released to the press.

Mr. McFarland nodded slowly as if he were giving Rich's question serious thought. "I know the sign you're talking about. A squiggly line intersecting a straight one. It's been talked about in the mountains for years."

"Have you ever seen it actually used by anyone or by a group of people?"

"I'm not sure what you mean by group of people."

"Like a biker gang or devil worshippers."

"We've had both of those around here, but I don't recall them using it."

"I'm thinking we saw that sign one day when we were fishing," Rich said. "It wasn't printed out like in the book. It was made out of twigs and maybe rocks if I remember right."

Mr. McFarland exhaled slowly and rubbed his bony fingers over his chin. "That was a long time ago. I didn't think you'd remember."

"I don't remember it too well. Where were we when you found me kicking those twigs?"

"Up at Craters River, at the end of the road that runs past the Fernhaven. I haven't been back there since. When the undead claim a spot, a smart man lets them have it."

"Wasn't there a campground up there somewhere?"

"There was. They closed it down after some college women got murdered in their sleep."

"So that's the campground where that happened."

"Yeah. Sad day that was. Somebody crossed a line they weren't supposed to cross. Don't go messing around in that area, Rich."

"Rest easy, Grandpa. I don't plan to rile any evil spirits."

"I know you think I'm just a superstitious old man, but I'm telling you, we're not the only ones on the planet. There are things out there with powers we can't begin to understand."

"Don't you worry about me, Grandpa. I got powers, too, right here on my hip."

"You be careful all the same. You, too, Deputy Fransen. You should really be careful, being a woman and all."

"I'll do that," she promised.

Rich's grandmother returned with the coffeepot and the talk of spirits and guns ceased. Unfortunately, it still consumed Carrie's thoughts.

BART HAD spent the morning checking out the wooded area around cabin twelve. There were footprints in the snow that led right up to the edge of the woods and then stopped in a spot that provided a good view of the cabin. At first he'd thought it might have been Jeff Matthews, but he'd checked out the bottom of his shoes when he'd crossed an ankle over his knee during lunch. The design in the soles didn't match.

But someone had been out there circling around like a wildcat; stalking and waiting for the moment when its prey was the most vulnerable. Someone who knew enough to keep anyone from following them back the way they'd come.

The prints had disappeared into the water and cracked ice that stood in the bottom of the ravine, the same ravine where Elora Nicholas's body had been dumped. Bart was certain that whoever was stalking the woods around the cabin was not on a nature walk. He was up to no good. Bart would stake his reputation as a cop on that.

His skills as a cop were all he was sure of these days. Katrina had his mind so messed up, he wasn't sure it would ever be straight again.

He took the woods back to the hotel, enjoying the solace and the sunshine that filtered through the evergreens and dappled the barren ground. He walked fast, hoping it would clear his mind of Katrina. It didn't. If anything the yearning to see her again grew stronger.

Once he'd reached the hotel, he cut across the employee parking lot and took the back way into the garden. Anticipation was already building, just on the chance that he might cross paths with her.

He cut through the hedges just north of the fountain. The old woman was there, but not Katrina.

"She needs you."

He looked around to see who the old woman was talking to, but there was no one but himself. He walked over and stopped beside her, so close to the fountain that the cold spray seemed to seep inside him.

"Were you talking to me?"

"Katrina needs you. You have to find her before it's too late."

"Too late for what?"

"Too late for her, and too late for you."

"If Katrina wants to see me, why isn't she here instead of you."

"She won't come to you. You must go to her."

"No. I don't play that kind of game."

"You must do it, if not for yourself or Katrina, then do it for Deputy Fransen. Do it now—or lose the chance forever."

Anger exploded inside him, as hot as the white pain of the bullet that had torn him apart. "Don't you dare drag Carrie into this."

"That is not my decision. Talk to Katrina, before it's too late for all of you."

"Where is she?"

"In the woods, on her way to the ravine. Go now, or lose her forever."

He took off at a run, leaving the woman behind. He didn't know what was going on, but he wouldn't let anything happen to Carrie. She was his partner, and a good cop never let his partner down.

He had just come from the area of the ravine east of the river. This time he went west. He found Katrina as soon as she left the path. She was just standing in the woods, staring into the distance, looking incredibly fragile and afraid.

When she looked at him, his resolve melted like a snowflake on the tip of a warm tongue. And in that second, nothing in this world could have stopped him from going to her and taking her in his arms.

Chapter Twelve

"Don't shut me out, Katrina. I'm trying hard to understand."

She went stiff in his arms. "This isn't about you, Bart. It's the necklace. It's gone."

"Your emerald pendant?"

"Yes, I had it in my pocket, and now it's not there."

"You must have dropped it. I'll help you find it."

"I've looked everywhere. There's no way to find something so small in the leaves and rocks." She trembled and collapsed onto a half-rotted tree stump. "It could be anywhere between here and the Fernhaven gazebo."

Bart hunched down beside her. He'd never thought of the pendant as small. "The necklace must be worth a small fortune."

"It's priceless. It was all in my hands, and now I've failed."

The last part of that was all he understood. He'd never been able to tolerate failure in himself. He still couldn't, which is why he was determined not to let his partner down.

The rest was as confusing as everything else Katrina had said lately. There had to be more than what she was saying. She could be involved in a theft ring, might even be the fence. Only why flaunt the pendant the way she had if it was stolen?

"Let's rehash this, Katrina. If you're 'not alive,' why does it matter so much that you've lost the necklace?"

"It's not just a necklace."

"So what is it?"

"It's...forget it, Bart. It's not your problem."

He fit a thumb beneath her chin and tilted it so that she had to look at him. Her eyes were moist, like emerald pools, and he felt that if he gave himself half a chance he'd drown in them.

And here he went again, thinking like a poet. The woman kept him so off balance, it was surprising he could walk.

"Tell me about the necklace, Katrina. I promise I'll do my best to understand."

"It's a family heirloom. My great-great-grandmother, Colleen, brought it with her when she came to America from Ireland. Her father had been murdered, and she and her mother stowed away on a cargo ship."

"That must have been a rough trip."

"Her mother died on the way over. Before she did, she gave Colleen the only thing of value she had."

"The necklace?"

"Yes. She was only fifteen, and she was in a new country, cold, hungry and all alone. She was terribly frightened."

"Why didn't she sell the necklace to buy food?"

"It was all she had of her mother's, and she was afraid that it was the necklace that had gotten her father killed. She didn't let anyone know she had it. She kept it hidden beneath her clothes, but always around her neck and close to her heart, at least that's the way the story was always told."

"So the jewelry stayed in the family, and you ended up with it?"

"The tradition was that it be passed down to the oldest daughter. And each one who wore it not only found happiness, but was empowered to rise above some great adversity. I know that sounds corny to you, but it's my heritage."

More than corny. It could have been a greeting card—or a country song. But there was no way to look into her eyes and not believe she was dead serious.

"My mother nearly lost her life when she was giving birth to me," Katrina continued. "The midwife told my father she'd never seen such suffering. But Momma held on to the necklace, and we both survived."

"If we find the necklace, will that give you back your life?"

"No, it's no longer for me. I must pass it on to my great-granddaughter. If I don't, it will be lost to our family forever."

"If you have a great-granddaughter, then you must have had a child when you burned to death in the hotel."

"I did, a daughter, born out of wedlock. I was the shame of my family, and people in our small town ostracized her because of my sins."

"Did you love her father?"

"No." She seemed to spit the word out. "No. I hated him. He was a teenage neighbor boy who came to our house to steal the necklace. I wouldn't give it to him, so he threw me to the floor and raped me. My mother came in while it was going on, and she shot and killed him."

"Good for her."

"We didn't think anyone would understand."

"Why not? A woman has a right to protect her daughter. It's always been that way in America."

"He was rich, and we were poor. That makes a difference when you seek justice. It's always been that way in America, too."

He couldn't argue that. "So what happened?"

"We buried him in the backyard."

If this was the kind of luck the necklace brought, Katrina should be thankful it was lost. So should her great-granddaughter. But Katrina wasn't glad. She was hurting. He could see her pain and feel it inside him as if it were his.

Whether the story was true or not, she believed it. And sitting here beside her as she relived the agony, it was difficult for him not to believe it, too.

"You must have been very brave."

"I wasn't brave at all. I was scared to death for nine months, and then my daughter was born. I named her Colleen after her ancestor. I loved her from the second I held her in my arms. She was smart and beautiful, and I treasured the necklace because I knew it had given her to me."

"Was Colleen with you at Fernhaven?"

"No. I was here on my honeymoon. She was with my mother."

Her honeymoon. He didn't know why that bothered him. It hit him then that he had begun to buy her strange story of having lived and died so long ago. She certainly talked the part. No one in his generation put words together quite like she did.

"I married for Colleen's sake," Katrina continued, "but I had hoped that my relationship with my husband would grow into love. Looking back, I doubt that would have happened, but I was young and I believed anything was possible."

Crazy, but he still believed that. If he didn't, how could he feel this way about a woman who told him she was dead without batting an eye? How could a woman decades older than him steal his heart? How could they have made love in a way that rocked his very soul?

"If you hadn't lost the necklace, how would you locate your great-granddaughter to give it to her?"

"She's staying in the hotel. The pendant brought her here. I don't know how exactly, but I'm sure that it did."

The confusion carousel started to spin again. "If she's here, why haven't you already put the necklace in her hands?"

"That's not the way it works. I can't speak with her unless she's receptive. I've followed her hour upon hour, stayed as close as I could, but I can't reach her."

"People in this world don't ordinarily do a lot of communicating with ghosts."

She jumped up and propped her hands on her slender hips. Her green eyes sparked with fire. "I'm not a ghost. I'm me, Katrina Ryan O'Malley." She stood and started to walk away.

He jumped up and caught her arm. "Don't go, please. I didn't mean to insult you."

"You doubt me when I tell you the truth."

"You're right. I'll stop doing that right now. I'll

change, but you have to change some, too. You have to realize how new all this is to me. Give me a chance. Give us a chance."

"There are no chances for us, Bart. I've told you that all along. I wish it could be different. I wish it so much. I've never known a man like you, never felt the way you make me feel."

"Then stay with me. Stop running away."

"There's so little time left."

"Let's not waste it. Make love with me again," he pleaded. "At least leave me with that."

"You don't make this easy."

"I want you so much it hurts, Katrina. If you want me, too, all you have to do is say so. How can it get any easier than that?"

"I do want you, but…"

He didn't wait for the but. He took her in his arms and kissed her. All he knew of life or death was that he wanted to be with Katrina. That was more than enough for now.

ANOTHER DAY had gone by without a note or an abduction. That was a good sign. It would have been a lot better if they were any closer to identifying the killer. They weren't. None of their efforts had produced any viable results and Harlan Grant was still avoiding the wide net that had been cast for him.

Carrie's high hopes for the frightening symbol

leading them to the killer were beginning to wane. Her fears were on the rise.

The possibility of an intersection between the living and the dead was chilling. So were an unexplained aura glowing through a photograph and an old woman running through a hotel trying to save guests from a fire that had been extinguished seven decades before.

But nothing was more frightening than a real live killer on the loose.

She went to the table in cabin twelve's small kitchen. Rich's endless lists were spread out like a fan. She picked up the top one.

Locals Familiar with the Layout of the Hotel.

There were several names on the list, two of which they'd already interviewed. One was the plumber who'd laid the pipes for the fountains. The second was Owen Billings.

They hadn't discussed this particular list before, but she'd ask Rich about it when he returned from his visit to Tom. She hoped that was soon. Maizie had called and said that Tom was asking to see him, and that it seemed urgent. Carrie couldn't wait to find out what that was about.

Odd to be wishing Rich was around when a few days ago she'd dreaded every conversation with him. But then she'd believed him to be a stubborn, arrogant cop. Actually, she still thought that, but he ran a lot deeper than her original assessment of him. Just how deep hadn't been determined.

She sighed. Spending time thinking about Rich McFarland's good qualities was a definite sign she was suffering from cabin fever. She got up and walked to the door, grabbing her parka and weapon as she went.

Wearing a gun was second nature to her now, but there had been a time when she'd shuddered every time she touched one. She'd come a long way as a deputy. This case was proving that she still had a long way to go.

HARLAN GRANT was watching when the female deputy stepped out of the cabin. She moved away from the door, but still in the glow of the outside light. She looked incredibly lonely. He knew that feeling well. Maybe they weren't so different after all.

She could be fantasizing right now, wishing she were with a real man. Her panties might be getting wet. Red thong panties. He'd thought about those a lot today. Thought about them so much that sometimes he'd forgotten that he'd created them in his mind. The deputy would be afraid at first, but when she realized he didn't mean to hurt her, she'd relax. And then he'd start to touch her and she'd get excited.

He'd have to take her by surprise, spring on her before she could pull her gun. He was ready, so ready.

C'mon, deputy. Make this easy on me. Walk this way. Follow the path until it skirts right by where I'm standing just like you did the other day.

She took a few steps in his direction as if she could hear him, as if she were thinking the same things that were running around in his mind. As if she wanted it just like he did.

He stripped off his gloves and stuffed them in his back pocket. He'd need his hands free.

She was closer now, only steps away. She pushed the hood of her parka back and turned all the way around as if she were listening for something.

He stooped and picked up one of the large rocks at his feet.

She was only three steps away. Two steps away. One step away.

And here!

CARRIE JERKED around, swinging her arm and blocking a blow to her head. She went for her gun, but the man was too quick. Before she could pull it, he'd wrapped his arms around her and pinned them to her side.

"Scream, and I'll kill you."

She twisted as much as she could, finally getting a glimpse of his face. "Harlan Grant."

"That's right."

"Then it was you who killed Elora?"

"No. I just want to be with you."

Carrie didn't plan to give him a chance. She yanked her elbows backward as hard as she could, but his hold on her held tight. He dragged her off the path and into the woods. But the gun was still at her waist. All she needed was half a chance, and she'd have it pointed at Harlan's head.

She dug her feet into the dirt.

"You aren't cooperating, deputy."

"I will. Stop here and I'll cooperate."

He kept dragging her. Carrie screamed, more to rattle him than in expectancy anyone would be close enough to hear.

Harlan threw her to the ground. She went for her gun, but he kicked her hand so hard that the gun slipped from her fingers, falling a few feet away.

She rolled toward it, almost getting her hands on it again before his foot landed in the small of her back, shoving her face into the frozen ground. He picked up the gun and pointed it at her.

"Take off your clothes."

"Never, you bastard."

"Take off your clothes or I'll take them off myself."

"The way you tore off Elora's before you killed her."

"I told you I didn't kill her. I've never killed anybody yet."

"Then why did you run?"

"'Cause you would have pinned it on me. That's

the way it works. I messed around and got into trouble. I got a problem, but I didn't kill nobody."

She had to buy time. She unzipped the parka and slipped it from one arm. Something crashed in the woods behind them. Harlan turned toward the sound.

Instinctively, she spun around, slinging the half-freed parka into his head at the same time she kicked the back of his knees, taking him down.

She jumped to her feet and took off running toward what she hoped was the cabin. If she moved through the trees fast enough, she'd make a poor target.

She could hear him behind her, gaining on her. His footfalls echoed in the night, sounding as if two or maybe more men were chasing her.

Her lungs burned, but she couldn't stop. If she did, she'd end up dead and Harlan Grant would escape again. She was not going to let that happen. But he was gaining on her and she was running as fast as she could on rough and rocky ground with trees blocking every path.

And then she heard a bloodcurdling shriek, as if someone's heart had been ripped out. The footsteps stopped.

She stretched her neck to see behind her. No one was there. She fell against a tree, struggling to catch her breath. Finally she saw Harlan, or at least she saw his head. He was a few feet behind her half-hidden in the trees, lying dead still.

She stepped closer. He was facedown and blood was pooling around his head. Using the toe of her boot, she nudged him over to his back. The blade of a knife was buried in his neck.

She knelt and felt for a pulse. There was none. Slowly it all sank in. She'd been saved by a freak accident. Harlan Grant had fallen on his own knife and killed himself.

IT WAS TWO in the morning before things had settled to anywhere near normal. Powell had brought two more deputies with him to help Carrie and Rich work the scene. Even though Harlan had killed himself, Powell wanted every tidbit of information he could get. Harlan's death was too closely tied to the larger investigation to let anything go overlooked. Fortunately, they also found her gun.

Finally, at a few minutes after one, they'd released Harlan's body for delivery to the morgue. At one-thirty Powell and the other two deputies had headed back to town.

Carrie had decided to make use of the cabin for the remaining few hours of the night, mainly because she was too weary to think about leaving. Rich opted to stay as well. She was glad. The guy was growing on her. She'd make sure he didn't find that out.

Now all she wanted was a hot, hot shower. She shed her clothes and stepped under the spray. Slowly her muscles started to relax. Unfortunately her mind didn't. She couldn't get the freak accident out of her mind. What were the odds that Harlan Grant would fall on his knife at that exact moment and that it would lodge in his neck?

If Fernhaven Hotel were haunted, it must have a few law enforcement friendly ghosts in residence.

She used one of the fluffy towels to dry off and slipped into the Fernhaven green terry robe the hotel provided. She made a turban of another towel and wrapped it around her wet hair. Tired as she was, she was still too wired to sleep, so she padded into the living room to see what kind of refreshment she could find in the minibar.

She chose a Merlot from Washington State.

Rich strode in from the other bedroom, still in his work uniform, and looking more haggard than she'd ever seen him.

"I thought you'd be sound asleep by now," he said.

"I'm still too keyed up. Join me in a glass of wine?"

"Sounds good. Here, let me open it." He took the corkscrew from its holder on top of the minibar and did the honors while she curled up in the easy chair next to the window.

He poured the wine and handed her a glass, holding his for a toast. "To the deputy of the day."

She clinked. "I didn't do a lot except almost get myself killed."

"Your methods were a little risky, but you got our man."

"Not according to him."

"Not unusual for a molester, rapist and killer to also be a liar."

"I guess." She wasn't totally convinced, but she might see things clearer tomorrow. "I almost forgot in all the excitement. What was it that Tom was so eager to discuss with you?"

Rich perched on the arm of the sofa nearest her chair. "He was finally ready to talk about what happened in the mountains."

"The day we found him or the day Maizie claims he saw whatever it was that blew his mind?"

"Both. They're related."

"That's a big development." She shed her slippers and tucked her feet into the chair with her. "What did he say?"

"Apparently some woman had approached him when he was in the mountains. She told him some bizarre story about having died in the fire that destroyed the original Fernhaven Hotel."

"No wonder he was freaked out."

"There was more. According to Tom, she begged

him to help her find someone in Seattle. She said she had to give him something."

"And she expected Tom to believe she'd hung around the mountains all those years?"

"Her explanation was that she'd been in some kind of transient state and only reentered this dimension with the rebuilding of the hotel. She had a limited time to do the task she'd been given, and then she'd leave this world forever."

"What did Tom tell her?"

"He said he was too stunned to react. He walked away, and when he turned back she was there one minute and then just disappeared."

A frigid knot settled in Carrie's chest. "Poor Tom."

"Yeah. Sad thing is, he still believes his hallucination was real. He claims he saw her again that day we found him. He said he offered to help her, but she told him it was too late. This time, she started to vaporize right before his eyes."

Carrie shivered, suddenly bone cold from the inside out.

"What do you make of that?"

"Tom's getting old, and he's lived with those fears and superstitions for so many years that they finally got the better of him."

The answer was too easy, or else Carrie was just too tired to think clearly tonight. She didn't want to believe in ghosts or disembodied spirits. But right now, she just couldn't be sure.

"What did Maizie say?"

"He hadn't told her. I suggested he not tell her or anyone else. At any rate, telling me and accepting it himself seems to have made a difference. He's making sense for the first time in two months, and that's good enough for Maizie."

But now the woman was on Carrie's mind. And so was Harlan Grant and the fall on the knife that couldn't have happened at a better moment.

Her mind went back to the symbol, and she doubted she'd get a wink of sleep tonight.

CARRIE AND RICH had spent the first two hours of the morning in meetings with hotel management explaining the situation that occurred on their property the previous night as best they could. It was obvious that management's main concern was to avoid any responsibility in Elora Nicholas's death.

But they had hired Harlan Grant without a background check, and Carrie was certain the press would run with that. Not that it was illegal to hire him. He'd done his time.

Carrie came out of the ladies' room and looked around the lobby for Rich. She found him on the phone. She caught his eye and made hand signals that she was going for coffee.

She got her latte to go, then carried it into the garden. The temperature wasn't much above freezing, but the sun was out, and there wouldn't be many more days like this until the spring.

The bench next to the fountain was empty. Carrie hesitated when the image from Jeff's photograph flew into her mind. She forced herself to sit down, but with the first sip of coffee, the hairs on the back of her neck seemed to stand on end.

She could have sworn someone was standing right behind her.

Her nerves were shot, she reasoned. That was all. The case had been a tough one, complicated by stories of ghosts and people who refused to die.

But the case was solved. The man who'd shot her partner was dead, and that gave her some very welcome closure. She needed just a bit more.

Carrie took out her pen and notebook, and each word she wrote felt as if it were a knife being plunged into Katrina's heart.

Chapter Thirteen

Dear Bart,
I never expected to have to face so much without you by my side. I was confused and shaken, at times almost debilitated by things I couldn't make sense of. I kept wishing you were here to ease my mind and make me laugh at myself.

I miss you, partner. I miss you very, very much.

Katrina backed away as tears filled her eyes and made it impossible to keep reading. It didn't matter. She'd read enough to realize that Carrie was in love with Bart. Why hadn't she seen that? How had she spent so much time near Carrie and never realized what was in her heart?

Katrina's only task, her only reason for existing in this dimension, was to deliver the pendant to Carrie. Instead she'd lost the necklace and made love with the man who'd been meant for her great-granddaughter. How could she be so irresponsible?

She'd been weak seventy years ago. She'd lain on the floor dying while Jonathan had started a fire that had killed over a hundred people. Now she was worse than weak. She was a failure in every way.

Bart belonged to Carrie. Katrina belonged to another world. It would claim her soon, the same way it would claim the few remaining guests of the original Fernhaven who'd been granted limited time to fulfill their earthly missions. The only thing she could do until that finality came was continue to search for the pendant and pray for a miracle. And stay away from Bart Finnegan.

She staggered away, consumed by a pain that had lodged in her soul. Losing Bart hurt more than the blow from her husband. More than the fire. More than death.

But if she had to do it all over again, she wouldn't hesitate for a second. One night in Bart's arms was easily worth an eternity of unrequited love.

CARRIE DIDN'T get away from the hotel nearly as early as she'd hoped. A group of the hotel's investors from Seattle were driving up and had requested a meeting with her, Sheriff Powell and Rich McFarland. So there was nothing to do but have lunch and stick around the hotel until they arrived.

The meeting didn't actually get started until three-thirty. By then Carrie had a splitting headache. Lack of sleep might not be the sole cause, but it was definitely a contributing factor. Rich noticed her downing pain pills and suggested she take his car and go home. He'd catch a ride with Powell.

Powell nodded his agreement. That was all the encouragement Carrie needed. It struck her as she drove out the gate that if she never came back to the Fernhaven Hotel, that might still be too soon.

Weariness set in big time as she started the drive home. With the fatigue came all the dark thoughts that had clouded her mind last night. The intersection of the undead and the living.

Had it happened to Tom? Could what he saw have been more than a bizarre and frightening hallucination?

Had Marjorie Lipscomb actually been visited by a woman who'd died in the hotel fire over seventy years ago?

Had Jeff Matthews captured phantasmal phenomena in the lens of his camera?

Had Selma intersected with a ghost who frightened her so badly she'd lost her grip on reality?

Carrie took a hand from the wheel and massaged the back of her neck. She was too tired to think.

That's why she was letting these frightening suspicions creep back into her mind.

It was over now. They had their killer. He'd denied it, but all the evidence pointed to Harlan Grant.

But if he'd killed Elora, why had he chosen that symbol as his signature? He had no ties to the superstitions of the mountains. He was from Kansas.

The doubts tumbled about in her troubled mind. She was dead tired, and the headache was almost blinding now. But the cold hard knot had settled in her stomach again and the symbol seemed to be searing itself into her brain.

She passed the sign for the cutoff road that led to the Billings's house. She fought a crazy urge to turn back and make another call on Selma. There were a dozen reasons why she shouldn't. The case was closed. Layers of foggy mist were already settling on the mountain. Carrie was dead tired and had a pounding headache.

But Selma had wanted to say more that day. Maybe now, with the case closed, she would. Carrie pulled onto the shoulder and made a U-turn. Call it crazy. Call it a hunch. But she wouldn't rest easy tonight unless she at least tried to talk to Selma.

THE DOGS that had met the car before didn't show up this time. Carrie waited a few minutes to make sure that they weren't just lying in wait or slow to spring into action. When there was still no sign of them, she crawled out of the car cautiously and started walking to the house.

She was already on the steps when she heard singing coming from around back. The song was haunting, the voice low but incredibly, sweet and clear.

"Selma. Is that you?"

There was no answer. Carrie made her way around the clapboard house, avoiding the weed-clogged flowerbeds and an upside-down washtub.

She rounded the back corner, then froze. Selma was there singing, and making a pattern in the grass with twigs and rocks.

Carrie leaned against the house for support. "What are you doing, Selma?"

"I'm making a Thanksgiving altar." She barely looked at Carrie. She just kept laying her pattern of twigs and singing her song.

She barely resembled the Selma of a few days ago. Her eyes glowed and her mouth was curved into a satisfied smile. And even though it was near freezing, she wasn't wearing a coat. All she had on was a thin skirt and a light blue sweater.

"Where's Owen?"

"He's not here."

"Where is he?"

"Where he always goes, I guess. He'll be back."

"Did he take the dogs?"

"They jumped in the back of his truck. He let

them stay." Selma placed another twig in the squiggly line, then twirled as if she were dancing.

"You seem happy today," Carrie said.

"Yes, very happy." She walked over to Carrie. "Would you like to know a secret?"

"Sure."

Selma rubbed her hands across her flat stomach. "I'm pregnant."

A new chill climbed Carrie's spine. She didn't even want to imagine how the symbol fit in with this news. "Does Owen know you're pregnant?"

"I told him. He's angry but he'll get over it. He always does."

"Doesn't he want a baby?"

"Not anymore. Not since…" She lowered her eyes. "You know."

"No. I don't know."

Selma started singing and went back to her Thanksgiving altar. Carrie walked over and took her hand. "Since what, Selma. What happened to change Owen's mind about having a baby?"

"Since I was with that man in the mountains."

Carrie's breath caught in her throat. "Was this someone you knew?"

"No. He just stepped out of the mist. I started to run, but he called my name and I stayed. He was beautiful and kind. When he touched me, it was like riding on a magic carpet with the whole world at your feet."

"Did you tell Owen about him?"

"Not at first, but then he saw the bruises."

"The man from the mist bruised you?"

"Yes, on my stomach, but it didn't hurt. Nothing he did hurt. The bruises are still here." She lifted her skirt and pulled down her panties. And there were the bruises—so pale Carrie could barely see them in the twilight, but still the pattern was clear. The intersection of the undead and the living.

"When did this happen, Selma? When did you first show the bruises to Owen?"

"A little over a month ago."

A month ago. Just before Elora was murdered. "Where's Owen?"

"He's not here." She picked up another twig from the stack she'd gathered.

Carrie yanked it away from her. "Listen to me, Selma. I have to find Owen. Where would you look if you needed him?"

"I don't know. He'll come back. He always comes back."

"That's not good enough. I need to find Owen now!"

"Then turn around, Deputy Fransen. I'm right behind you."

She turned and stared down the long barrel of a shotgun.

THE WEST WING at Fernhaven was officially opening for business the next day. Fine with Bart. Fancy resorts weren't his bag anyway. He gave his old room no more than a parting glance as he stepped into the hall.

He'd done what he'd set out to do. He'd stood by his partner. He'd gotten no credit for taking the knife from Harlan and killing him with it, but that didn't matter. Sometimes it was best that way. Now it was time to move on, to start a new life and leave the old one behind.

A month ago the thought of that would have been more than he could bear. A lot had changed since then. He'd changed. Part of the difference could be attributed to his taking the bullet. Most of it was due to Katrina.

He didn't understand her but who ever understood women? Her talk of death was disturbing, but when they made love, heaven and earth seemed to merge, so it didn't matter a whole lot to him which one she thought they were in. Besides, he'd get her help. What love couldn't accomplish, counseling and time surely could. All he knew for certain was that he loved her more than he'd dreamed possible, and he wasn't going to lose her.

"Well done."

He spun around. It was the old woman. It creeped him out the way she seemed to appear out of nowhere. "What was well done?"

"Your task."

"What task?"

"You saved Carrie."

How in the devil could she know that? "Who are you?"

"The taskmaster."

More like resident fruit cake. But she'd gotten his attention. "What does a taskmaster do?"

"I'm here to make certain all the spirits trapped in this dimension understand their tasks and their limitations."

"And do these spirits always do as you tell them?"

"No. Some are as irresponsible in death as they were in life. Others simply don't understand. And a few are stopped by factors beyond their or my control."

The talk made him uneasy, and he wondered if she was the one who had Katrina confused. If so, he'd find a way to keep the two of them apart. "Have you seen Katrina?"

"Sit down, Bart. We need to talk."

"About Katrina?"

"Yes, and about you."

"I don't have time. I'm looking for Katrina."

"That can wait. This can't."

CARRIE FELT every bump and swerve as they rattled along the curving mountain road. Her feet and ankles were bound and a red mechanic's rag had been shoved to the back of her throat, making it painful to swallow and impossible to talk. She was on the floor, stuffed behind the seat in the cab of Owen's truck like a piece of excess luggage or a pair of old boots. She could see the gun rack above her and the back of Owen's head.

She couldn't see Selma's head at all, but she could hear her from time to time, singing the same haunting tune she'd been singing when Carrie had found her building the pattern of twigs. It was about life and death and making love.

Owen was mumbling the way he'd been doing ever since Selma had helped him tie the ropes around Carrie's hands and feet. Carrie couldn't understand half of what he said, but what she understood was enough to turn her inside out.

"Violated. Deconsecrated. Tainted by the devil. Did you know that, Deputy?"

He was rattling on, knowing Carrie couldn't answer with the rag stuffed in her mouth.

"Damaged goods. Damaged. Damaged. Filth growing inside her."

Selma kept singing, as oblivious to his remarks as she'd been back at the house when she'd obeyed his every command. They were both stark-raving mad. There would be no reasoning with either of them.

For a few minutes back there, Carrie had thought she might be going mad as well. But the pieces were falling into place now. Owen had probably gone to the bar in the hotel to drink away his anger and hurt over his wife's infidelity.

Elora and her husband must have argued while he was there. Already going out of his mind, he'd followed her from the bar, then accosted her before she reached her room.

He must have dragged her through the woods and tried to cross the road so that they were farther away from the cabins. But then he'd run into Bart and doubled back to the ravine not all that far from cabin twelve.

"Impregnated by the devil."

Owen was angry, revolted by what his wife had done. He might have forgiven the indiscretion over time, but he would never get over the pregnancy.

He didn't have any intention of letting Selma have this baby. That's why he'd brought her along. He planned to kill both of them which meant that Carrie had more than herself to save.

But two against one was way better odds than one against two. All she had to do was make Selma see that Owen was going to kill her, if they didn't stop him first.

But Selma was still singing, lost in a world whose axis revolved around an intersection between the living and the dead.

RICH TRIED his cell phone. No signal. Par for the course for this part of the county. About once a day, he managed to get coverage from the hotel, and then it was usually so weak he got little more than static. He gave up and headed for the phone booths in the corridor just off the main lobby. They'd be clearer then his squawk box in the car.

The meeting with the hotel's investors had officially come to a close, but Powell was still in there talking the ears off of a couple of the guys who'd started out by thinking they could give him orders.

Money and position might talk in the circles they usually ran in, but the sheriff was half-deaf all the time and totally deaf to anything that hinted of intimidation.

There were four phones, only one of which wasn't in use. He took it and called Carrie's cell phone number. It rang until the voice mail message came on. He hung up without leaving one, but he got that annoying little acid drip in the pit of his stomach.

She should be home by now, but she wouldn't have turned her cell phone off. It was the only phone she owned. But she might have fallen asleep. There was nothing to worry about. The perp was dead.

There was just that one nagging question that hadn't been answered and that he hadn't wanted to mention to Carrie just yet. How was Harlan connected to the symbol that had been cut into Elora's stomach?

Rich stepped back from the phone booth, reached

into his shirt pocket and pulled out the list he'd started on the drive back from Tom's last night.

Locals who know the hotel and who've reported dealings with the spirits.

There was only one name on the list so far. Owen Billings, and his dealings with spirits hadn't come directly. They'd come through his wife, and Harlan hadn't admitted that. But Selma had said something to Maizie or else Maizie had assumed that the mountains had sent Selma spiraling into depression a couple of months after she'd miscarried.

Rich tried Carrie's number again. Still no answer. If this were a TV detective show, the car would have a GPS system, and he'd be able to track the location of the vehicle and make certain she was home. His car was lucky to have a radio.

While he was standing at the phone and waiting on the sheriff, he might as well call and check on Tom. Tom answered on the first ring.

"Where are you?" Tom asked. "I've been trying to call you for ten minutes."

"The dead-cell zone. What's up?"

"Maizie just made me take her over to the Billings's to check on Selma. Nobody was there, but I would have sworn that was your old wreck parked in front of the house."

"It could have been. Carrie was driving it home from the hotel. Are you sure no one was there?"

"Not a soul. We walked all around the house and even peeked in the windows. The house was dark."

"Thanks for the info. I'll check it out."

"One more thing. There was this symbol in the backyard, laid out in twigs and rocks. It was…"

The acid drip turned into a raging river as Rich cut Tom off and ran to get the sheriff. No wonder Harlan hadn't matched with the symbol. He wasn't their man.

Somehow Carrie had figured that out and now she was out there facing the real madman all alone. And he could have taken her anywhere, anywhere at all.

TWILIGHT HAD deepened to a hoary gray when Owen's pickup truck made a jerking stop. Owen killed the engine and opened his door.

No time for panic, Carrie reminded herself. It was crunch time, and she'd trained for this moment for years. And if there were supernatural powers to face, she'd find a way to do that, too.

"Get out of the car, Selma."

"Stop it, Owen. You're hurting me."

"Then do what I say."

Selma whimpered, but she must have complied. A second later the front passenger seat flew forward.

"Your turn, pretty deputy." Owen took hold of her feet and pulled her close enough that he could reach in and grab her arm. He yanked her up, then dragged her out of the truck, leaning her against the front fender.

There wasn't much she could do with her hands and feet tied except try to get a feel for where they were. Nothing looked familiar. Selma started singing again, this time it was a lullaby.

Owen grabbed Carrie and started dragging her into the woods. Her feet scraped and bumped along the ground as if she were a dead weight. She couldn't see far in the growing darkness, but she could hear Selma following behind them.

"I want to go home," Selma begged between songs.

But they kept walking until Selma quit singing and started to cry.

"Just a few more steps. We're almost there, almost to the ravine," Owen said.

Carrie looked around. She spotted the ravine and the downed tree in the twilight and knew they were at the same spot where they'd found Elora's body.

"Okay, pretty deputy. This is the end of the road." Owen stooped down and cut the rope from her feet, then yanked the rag from her mouth. Her hands were still tied in front of her and his grip on her arm was so firm, she couldn't break away.

If he was going to kill her here, there was only one reason for him to have cut the rope on her ankles. Now he'd be able to separate her legs. Her stomach rolled sickeningly, but she forced herself to hold on to control.

"Scream all you want now, Deputy. No one will hear you, and if they do, they'll just think you're a screech owl out looking for dinner." He pulled a hunting knife from his pocket.

Selma grabbed his arm. "What are you doing?"

"Nothing. Get back and shut up." He shook his arm free, and Selma cowered next to him.

"He's going to kill me, Selma. He's going to rape me and slice my throat the same way he did Elora Nicholas. And when he's through with me, he's going to kill you."

"Shut up, you bitch. I should have left the rag in your mouth."

"He's going to kill us both, Selma, unless you help me stop him. You'll never get to have your baby."

Owen slapped Carrie so hard across the face that her vision went blurry. When she could see again, she saw Selma. She'd pulled up her shirt and was staring at her stomach.

"You can't hurt my baby," she wailed. "I won't let you do that, Owen."

He glanced at her bared stomach and then it was as if something exploded inside him. He shoved Carrie to the ground and grabbed Selma.

Something hard dug into Carrie's knee. She picked it up. It was some kind of necklace, bulky and covered in mud. But its sharp points were the closest thing she had to a weapon.

When she looked back, she knew it wouldn't be enough. Owen had Selma on the ground, and he was holding the knife to her stomach.

Carried screamed at him to stop, but he plunged the knife into his wife's stomach as if he were gutting a fish. There was no time to wait, no chance at reason. Carrie dived on Owen. She pulled him backward as best she could with her hands tied, but he was too strong. He rolled her over and pinned her to the ground.

Now the knife was at her neck.

She was going to die, but she'd die proud. She might have no roots, but she had herself. She was Deputy Carrie Fransen, and she'd die fighting to the end.

Bart would be proud of her.

So would Rich. He wasn't half-bad as a partner. Now she wished she'd told him so.

Chapter Fourteen

Rich was running on an adrenaline rush and a prayer, following nothing more than raw gut instinct. If Owen had killed Elora, then he might return to the same place. It happened occasionally, especially when the killer wasn't your normal criminal type.

It was nearly dark when Rich hit the woods, but still light enough that he didn't have to turn on his flashlight to maneuver through the trees. That made it better than Bart had had it the night he was shot.

Rich pushed the thought to the back of his mind. That night had ended in death. This one wouldn't. Carrie was trained and smart. She'd know how to handle Owen.

Still dread pummeled inside him as he rushed toward the spot where Elora's body had been dumped in the old ravine. If Owen hurt Carrie, he'd kill him with his bare hands.

A man's voice carried on the night breeze. Rich was almost sure it was Owen's. His chest tightened, but he kept a steady finger on the trigger of his weapon as he crept closer.

And then he saw them and his insides kicked so hard, Rich felt it clear to his heart. Owen was taunting Carrie, letting the blade of his knife slide over her flesh at the point of her jugular vein. A little more pressure on the knife, and...

No. He wasn't going to let it happen. But even if Rich put a bullet though Owen's head, the push from the guy's reflexes alone might be enough to bury the blade in Carrie's throat.

"I didn't want to kill Elora," Owen said, his voice easily carrying to where Rich was hidden in the trees. "I don't want to kill you. It's the mountains. They're making me do it. The mountains and Selma."

Owen's voice was shaking, and so were his hands. He'd lost it and Rich damn sure couldn't just wait around. He stepped from behind the trees. "You have until three to drop the knife, Owen. I'm starting counting with two."

Owen turned, but only for an instant. That was all it took. Carrie swung her right hand into Owen's face, striking his left eye with what looked like a piece of metal. He fell backward, yelping like an injured dog and clawing at his eye while blood poured down his face.

But the knife was still in his hand, and Carrie was still pinned beneath him with her hands bound at the wrists. Owen lifted his hand to strike, and Rich pulled the trigger. Owen went down. The knife missed Carrie by a fraction of an inch.

Rich rushed over and shoved Owen's dead weight off of her. His chest was so tight, he had to fight for breath before he could speak. "Are you all right?"

"Yeah. About time you got here, partner. A deputy could die waiting on you to show up."

He breathed a little easier as he helped her to her feet and cut the rope from her wrists. "It's your own damn fault, Fransen. Didn't anyone ever tell you to let your partner know what you're up to?"

"Next time," she said. "Next time."

He'd never been so thankful in his life that there could be a next time.

BART HURRIED down the hotel corridor. It had been a harrowing two nights. Carrie had come close to losing her life twice. Once he'd saved her. Harlan Grant had never seen him coming and never had a chance against him.

Tonight Carrie's new partner had been the one to step up to the plate. He guessed that was fitting. It was time for Bart to let go, and it was nice to know he was leaving her in good hands.

Carrie would do just fine. She was on her way to

becoming one hell of a deputy. She was already one hell of a woman.

The ballroom was dark and deserted when Bart pushed through the door. It seemed the party was over and the dancers had all gone home. He was ready to go himself, but first he had to find Katrina.

He stood in the middle of the empty dance floor, thinking of the night he'd first looked into her mesmerizing eyes. He'd fallen in love with her then and there. He just hadn't known it.

He knew it now. Finally he understood a lot of things he'd never grasped before. The taskmaster had handed it to him straight. Apparently it was her job to assist those who were too hardheaded to accept things as they were.

Bart was a lot smarter now about life and death, but mostly about love.

The clock struck the bewitching hour. On the last tone, Katrina walked through the door, dressed the same as she'd been the first night he'd seen her, except that the necklace was no longer around her neck.

He walked over and took her hands in his. "May I have this dance?"

"I can't." Her voice shook and she kept her eyes cast downward. "I've come to say goodbye, Bart."

He backed away, hurt and bewildered. "What are you saying?"

"We can't stay together."

"Of course, we can. I understand everything now. I know you have to go, but I'm going with you."

Finally, she gave him one quick glance. "Oh, Bart. Please don't make this so hard. We were never meant to be together. If we try, it will be all wrong."

"Wrong? How can you say that? We're perfect together, and you know it. Look me in the eyes and tell me you don't want to be with me forever."

She met his gaze. Her eyes were wet with tears.

"I love you, Bart. I never knew what love was when I was alive and never dreamed it was possible to find it now."

"And I love you, so quit talking crazy."

"I'm talking the truth—that's all. You belong with Carrie. She's your destiny, not me. I can't change that, and I won't."

"Carrie Fransen?"

"Yes. I didn't know about the two of you at first, but now that I do, I can't come between you."

"Whoa. You've lost me totally. How do you even know Carrie?"

"She's my great-granddaughter."

Damn! He'd only thought he had this straight. "Do you mean that Carrie Fransen is the person who was supposed to inherit the necklace?"

"Yes. I failed her, but I won't betray her."

"If Carrie is the one you were trying to get the necklace to, then you didn't fail her. She found it tonight, apparently where you'd lost it."

"Don't humor me, Bart."

"I'm not. I was there, too late to help, but I was there. I know this sounds unbelievable, but Carrie accidentally fell on the necklace near the ravine. She used it to fight off the man who killed Elora Nicholas and who shot me. I followed Sheriff Powell to the scene of the crime and stayed around until I'd heard it all."

Finally, she smiled. "Oh, Bart. Do you know what that means?"

"Probably not. I still seem to be missing the mark a lot."

"The necklace hasn't lost its powers. It fell in Carrie's hands miraculously in spite of my ineptitude. She'll be empowered, and the necklace will stay in our family to touch women's lives for generations to come."

"Right now, that necklace is the least of my concerns." He wrapped his hands around her forearms and held on tightly so that she couldn't run away or disappear on him. "I don't know what you heard about me and Carrie, but you've got it wrong. We were close, close as partners could get. She was even infatuated with me for a while, but she got over it."

"No. She misses you so much."

"And I miss her. We were a team, but we were never *in love*, and we never made love."

"But in her notes…"

Bart let go of her arms and cradled her sweet face in his hands. "Look at me, Katrina. I've spent my whole life moving toward this moment, moving toward you. I'll accept whatever comes next. All I ask is that I step into eternity with you. Only you."

She smiled through her tears and lay her head on his shoulder. "In that case, Bart Finnegan, you may have this dance."

Epilogue

Rich watched as Carrie knelt at Bart's tombstone and lay the handful of daisies on his grave.

"We got him, Bart. It took us awhile, but we got the man who killed you, just like I promised we'd do."

Rich gave her a few minutes alone, then walked over and joined her. He lay a hand on her shoulder. "You still miss him, don't you?"

"I'll always miss him, but I'm still thankful I had the opportunity to know him and to work with him." She stood and ran her hand along the smooth marble of his tombstone. "I've tried a million times to think of what it must have been like for him, dying all alone in the woods that night."

"The good thing was he had to have died instantly from Owen's bullet, so he didn't have time to do a lot of thinking."

"If he lived even a second, he'd have been furious with himself for not stopping the suspect and saving Elora. He was that kind of deputy, true to his cause all the way."

"That's the mark of a real police officer."

She wrapped her arms about her chest. "I'm glad the case is finally over," she said, "and especially relieved Selma wasn't pregnant. She'll have a much better chance of recovering from all this without that. Not to mention that she was in no condition to become a mother."

"No, she's in the right place now," Rich agreed. "Hospital care is what she needs. Woman had to be sick to bruise herself that way and then claim to be pregnant."

"She never admitted to putting those bruises on herself," Carrie reminded him. "She still claims that she made love to one of the undead in the mountains and that he left his mark on her."

"The symbol that drove Owen to kill Elora and to come damn close to killing you. That's what I hate about these mountain superstitions. They get in people's heads and just don't let go."

"Things have calmed down at Fernhaven," Carrie said. "Chuck says the complaints of ghostly noises and happenings have all but stopped."

"After the hotel's been opened for another year or so, they'll probably stop completely. It's just the history of the place and the abduction that had people imagining things."

"Maybe. I'm still not as convinced as you are that supernatural events didn't have a bearing on the crime and our investigation."

"And who knows, maybe you're right. I never claimed to know it all."

She looked at him and raised her eyebrows.

He grinned. "Not all—just *almost* all."

She punched him lightly on the arm, then fingered the silver chain around her neck. The pendant itself was hidden beneath her uniform shirt, but Rich was sure it was there. It always was. "Did you get a final word on the necklace?"

"Yes. The hotel researched their records. If claims on the necklace were ever filed, they've long since been lost. It officially belongs to me, my good luck piece to pass down to posterity. I may not have roots, but I'll make some."

"That's fitting since the pendant saved your life."

"You saved my life, Rich. The pendant merely slowed Owen down when the edge of the setting tore out his eye."

"What can I say? I'm a hell of a cop."

"Then we should make a terrific team."

He nodded and smiled in spite of himself. "We're getting there, Fransen. We are definitely getting there."

If you enjoyed what you just read,
then we've got an offer you can't resist!

Take 2 bestselling love stories FREE!

Plus get a FREE surprise gift!

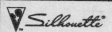

INTRIGUE

Don't miss this first title in Lori L. Harris's exciting new Harlequin Intrigue series—

THE BLADE BROTHERS OF COUGAR COUNTY

TARGETED

(Harlequin Intrigue #901)

BY **LORI L. HARRIS**

On sale February 2006

Alec Blade and Katie Carroll think they can start fresh in Cougar County. Each hopes to bury the unresolved events of their violent pasts. But they soon learn just how mistaken they are when a faceless menace reappears in their lives. Suddenly it isn't a matter of outrunning the past. Now they have to survive long enough to have a future.

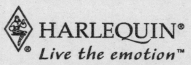

HARLEQUIN®
Live the emotion™